Nava

A Tale of Redemption

D. P. Conway

Part of
The Christmas Collection

Day Lights Publishing House, Inc.

Cleveland, Ohio

From Darkness to Light through the Power of Story

The Christmas Collection

Go to Series Page on Amazon

or

Search DP Conway Books

Did you receive this as a gift? Please post a review on AmazonYou can reach Dan at authordpconway@gmail.com

Dedications

For Marisa
Thank you for helping me to keep Christmas well.
Io Ti Amo Sempre.

For Patrick
Keep Leading the Way

For my biggest fans, my children,
Colleen, Bridget, Patrick, and Christopher.

For my littlest fans,
my little Aubrey
and my little Avery.

For Christine

For Mary Grace

Chapter 1

Bethlehem, Judea

The screaming in the village had already started. Nava peered over the courtyard wall of her lifelong friend Leah's home. Leah's husband was lying on the ground just inside the home, next to the back door. His midsection was blood-stained. He was dying. Nava held her hand to her mouth, terrified.

The next moment, she saw Leah crouched in the opposite corner of the courtyard in front of her children, fending off a Roman soldier. Her arms were spread wide, frantically moving, trying to protect little Gabrielle and Gershon as they hid behind her, screaming in fright.

"No! No! Please, no!" Leah screamed, her face pleading in anguish, her body maneuvering in any way to shield them.

The soldier had his back to Nava, so she quickly placed the sword on top of the wall and then struggled to climb up and over.

She was halfway up when she saw the soldier turn his sword and strike Leah in the head with the handle of it. Leah fell backward, barely conscious. The soldier reached for the crying little boy, but Leah rose. "No!! She cried as she attacked him, biting his arm.

The soldier knocked her off and lifted his sword high, readying it. Finally, Nava crested the wall and jumped down, landing softly, carrying Aaron's sword in hand. She lifted it high and ran straight at the unsuspecting soldier.

Chapter 2

Three years earlier

Aaron ran as fast as he could. His slightly clubbed foot caused him to move slower than other young men his age, but he was used to it now, and to him, it was not even noticeable. He was coming from his home on the eastern edge of Bethlehem toward the country road that led to the hidden caves on the hills on the outskirts of the small village.

Farmers sometimes used these caves as small stables, but most were abandoned this time of year. There was a broad field across from the caves, and that was where, in particular, he was going. He was on his way to see his new friend and had to be careful, as he was not supposed to be friends with this man. His friend was the leader of a Roman unit camped in the field for the last two months.

Aaron left the confines of town and headed into the brush, some hundred yards off the road. He did not want anyone to see him going up the road. It might raise questions or start rumors that could get his family in trouble with the elders of Bethlehem. The Romans were the sworn enemies of many in Bethlehem, as they were in all of Judea. But for Aaron, it was not so. They had never done anything to him, and even growing up, though he heard about how hard the Roman occupation was, it did not seem to affect his daily life.

He had just turned eighteen. Aside from his permanent limp, which he had since he had learned to walk as a toddler, he was strong and ruddy. He was medium height, with dark black hair, tan skin, and dark brown eyes, and his smile was kind and a glimpse into his heart.

He did not believe that he or his people were doomed just because the Roman Empire reigned over Judea. Yes, they were the occupiers of practically the whole world, but who would ever know in Bethlehem? Aaron had not seen more than a handful of Roman soldiers passing through in the last several years.

They never stayed.

This group, this unit as his friend called themselves, was only here because of news of bandits operating to the south of Bethlehem.

He reached the top of the ridge where the road crested, went a little farther, and then crossed back onto the road. He would not be visible from the town any longer. In the distance, he saw some soldiers milling around the Roman encampment. Aaron marveled at their shiny, colorful uniforms. He wished he could be a soldier instead of a lowly shepherd.

He slowed his pace, knowing from experience it was not wise to run up unexpectedly to a Roman Army unit. He had made this mistake the first time and was greeted with drawn swords and angry, concerned faces. Only the leader, now his friend, had acted quickly to call them off and allow Aaron to approach.

It was the beginning of their friendship.

Aaron said to the soldier nearest the entrance to their encampment. "Hi, Quintus. Is Claudius able to see me?"

The soldier smiled, "He had a feeling you might drop by today." He motioned over his shoulder. "He's back there tending to his horse."

"Thanks, Quintus."

Aaron walked into the encampment and past several tents, nodding to some of the soldiers, most of whom acknowledged him. They liked Aaron, because he did not resent them like most of the people in Bethlehem. They also appreciated that he had brought them unleavened bread several times. He had procured discreetly by bartering with his friend's mother in exchange for helping her with some field tasks.

Aaron spotted Claudius, the leader of the twenty-man unit. He was standing in his full uniform, except for his helmet, and brushing his black horse down.

"Hello, Claudius!" Aaron said.

Claudius glanced over his shoulder, keeping the brush strokes going, "Well, good afternoon, Aaron. How are you today?"

"I am doing well. I just came from helping my father work in the fields."

"I see. You're a good man to help your father. How is Nava doing?"

Aaron smiled widely, "She is well, Claudius. She enjoyed meeting you and said she will return with me soon."

"She's a lovely young lady. I am happy for you both. When are you going to marry?"

"In the springtime."

Claudius kept brushing but turned to meet Aaron's eyes, smiling, "That will be the beginning for you, Aaron. It will be the start of life."

"Thank you, Claudius."

"Are you married?"

"I lost my wife to illness seven years ago." He stopped for a moment, seemingly lost in thought, and lowered his head for a brief moment, closing his eyes."

"I'm sorry, Claudius."

Claudius exhaled and began brushing again. "It's never easy, Aaron. Cherish your bride. Cherish her always because long life is not promised to all."

There was quiet for a few moments as Claudius continued brushing the shiny coat of his horse. Aaron broke the silence. "I'm sorry, I don't have any bread today. I had no time to procure it."

Claudius laughed, reaching higher onto the back of his horse, brushing towards the back now. "Don't worry about us, Aaron. We have plenty to eat."

Claudius was quiet, unusually quiet.

"Why are you brushing your horse?" Aaron asked. "I've never seen you do this."

"Well, I wanted to talk to you about something."

"What is it?"

"Well, we are leaving very early tomorrow." Claudius stopped and turned, tight-lipped. "I just found out this morning. I was hoping you would come by so I could tell you."

"Really," Aaron said, his face drawn downward, "Will you be coming back?"

"Perhaps. There is trouble in Jerusalem, and the Tribune wants us to join back up with our Legion."

"What kind of trouble?"

Claudius sighed, "There are a lot of people who do not like Roman laws, Aaron. Our job is to uphold Roman law and justice throughout the Empire."

Claudius stopped brushing his horse. "Come with me, Aaron."

Claudius walked a few yards away, set down his brush, and sat on a log. "Sit down."

Aaron sat.

"I have a gift for you." Claudius reached behind the log and lifted a gold-handled sword.

Aaron's eyes widened.

"This is for you, Aaron. I hope you will remember me by it. I have enjoyed our brief friendship."

Aaron took the sword in his hand, carefully turning it, marveling at it. "Oh, this is so amazing. Thank you, Claudius."

Claudius patted him on the shoulder, "You're welcome."

Aaron looked up, "I wish we had an army…. I mean, I wish I could be a soldier. It seems like such an exciting life."

"Aaron, being a soldier is hard and not for everyone. I have had to kill some men in battle and in defense of our mission. Killing someone changes you. It makes you… Well, it makes you wonder about life and death. It makes you… Sad, I guess."

Aaron lowered his head. "I never thought of that."

"It's not something anyone thinks about until it happens."

Nothing was said between them for a few minutes.

Claudius broke the silence. "I hope you can use this sword for good, Aaron. To defend your family someday. To bring honor to yourself."

Aaron stood, brandishing it slowly. "I will try, Claudius. Thank you."

Claudius stood and hugged him tightly. "Take care of yourself, young man. Perhaps we will see each other again."

Chapter 3

Aaron took the sword to one of the nearby caves, which none of the shepherds used. He made sure no one was around, then went inside and hid the sword near the back of the cave. He came out of the cave slowly to make sure no one was near, then ran down the hillside, careful to stay off the road until he reached the village. Then he headed down the main village road to Nava's house.

Nava was sitting out front of her family's home, turning the grinder to grind the wheat into flour. Aaron slowed, limping slightly and quietly, wanting to admire her before she saw him. She wore her white tunic that extended to near her beautiful sandal-covered feet. Her hair was deep brown and hung naturally over one shoulder, and she labored to turn the grinding tool. Her light blue mantle was next to her, neatly folded.

Aaron walked a little closer, then stood about twenty feet before her, with his arms crossed, smiling, watching her, waiting for her to look up. Finally, she did.

"Aaron," she said, surprised, as a wide, loving smile crossed her face.

"Good morning, Nava," he said as he approached her. She stood, brushing the grain from her tunic, and they embraced warmly. "I missed you," Nava said.

"You just saw me yesterday," said Aaron.

Nava laughed, "I know, but I still missed you. I can't wait to spend every day and night together."

Aaron put his finger over his mouth, signaling for quiet. He glanced over her shoulder, peering into the house to make sure her parents were not near, then took hold of her shoulders and pulled her close, kissing her softly.

They pulled apart slowly, and then both laughed, feeling like children, though they would marry in the Spring.

"I have something to show you," Aaron said.

"What is it?" she asked.

"Come with me."

Nava returned her grinding tools, wheat kernels, and ground flour to the house. "Mama, I will be back soon. I have to help Aaron with something."

"Don't be long," came the reply from her mother, Rachel, who was in the back of the house feeding the chickens.

~ ~ ~ ~

When they reached the cave, Aaron retrieved the sword; he came out with the shiny sword lying across his outstretched arms.

Nava's eyes widened, and she covered her mouth, "Where did you get this?"

"Claudius gave it to me. They are leaving tomorrow, and he wanted me to have it as a gift. Here, hold it."

Nava took the golden sword handle and then held the shiny sword aloft. "It's not that long or heavy," she said.

"No, Claudius told me once that they use shorter swords for close-range combat. This must be one of them."

"It's amazing," Nava said as she stepped back and gently thrust it up, down, and across. She looked up, "What will you tell your parents?"

"I'm not sure. I will keep it hidden until we are married. Then we can bring it into our home."

"I want to learn how to use it," Nava said.

Aaron's lips pursed for a moment as he considered her and smiled. "I can teach you, but we must do it secretly."

"Okay," Nava said.

Aaron held the sword aloft, then said, "I will get some proper wooden sticks, and we can carve handles on them, then begin tomorrow."

"Oh, that sounds fun," Nava said, stepping to him, embracing him, and kissing him again.

Chapter 4

Over the next several weeks, Nava and Aaron met secretly at the cave and practiced with fashion sticks. Until one day, Aaron came with a real sword. He let Nava use the Roman sword Claudius had given them, and they practiced. The sound of real steel clanging loudly surprised Nava; it even scared her. The thought of real men using these weapons to kill each other was frightening. Still, she wanted to learn, for she imagined someday needing to protect her family or even teach her own children about swords.

They finished their first real practice session. Aaron put the sword back in the cave and set off together to a nearby stream to rest.

Aaron dangled his feet in the stream as Nava sat back slightly, not wanting to let her feet touch the water. "Nava," he said, "We come from a very special village. Just think, there are only a few thousand people in Bethlehem, and so many famous were born here. Do you know them all?"

"Of course I do," Nava said.

"Okay, tell me."

"Well, there is King David, of course. My Grandfather Caleb said when he was a boy, his grandfather knew some of the direct descendants."

"Amazing. Who else?"

"Well, then there is Jacob, whose beloved wife Rachel had died and was buried in Bethlehem."

"Yes, she was a great woman of faith."

"Is there anyone else?" Aaron was only asking her because he was waiting for her to recount someone else, someone he would be sure they talked about today, even if Nava did not recall them.

Nava blushed, lowering her eyes, "You know my favorite people from Bethlehem."

"Hmmm... who are you talking about?"

"Ruth and Boaz, of course."

Boaz and Ruth had lived in Bethlehem when they were young lovers. Nava and Aaron had visited their old farm near the outskirts of the village right before they had become betrothed to one another.

"Come on. It's not far," Aaron said, jumping up and helping her. They ran for over a mile until they finally reached the hilltop overlooking what was known to be Boaz's old farm. They sat in the grass, surveying the beautiful horizon in the distance. Aaron said to her, "Can you imagine, Nava? This is the field where Boaz first laid eyes on Ruth."

"I know," Nava said tenderly, "It is one of my favorite stories."

Aaron took her by the hand, "It is here too that I first professed my love for you, Nava. He stood, knelt beside her, taking her hand, "And I profess my love for you again today. I will always love you, just as Boaz always loved Ruth."

Nava stood as they pulled each other up. She rested her head on his shoulder, then lifted her chin and kissed him warmly. As they gently pulled away, they turned and looked out at the horizon, feeling a surge of hope, the kind only young lovers could understand.

She exclaimed," Someday, Aaron, they will remember us too. Our love story will be remembered and talked about, just like we remember Boaz and Ruth."

As they headed down the hill, back toward their homes in the village, Nava realized that this day was the happiest day of her life so far and one she would never forget.

Chapter 5

Several weeks later, on a cool September evening, there was a loud knock at the front door. Nava turned to her mother, Rebecca, then leaned over to peer out the window.

She frowned and said, "Uncle Erez is here."

Rebecca stood up quickly, moved the vegetables she was cleaning to the side, and took off her apron, shouting, "Get the door, Nava."

Nava sighed. She did not like Uncle Erez.

He was her Father's older brother and acted like he was the boss of the family. She knew full well that her Grandfather Caleb was still the head of their family, but he was getting up in years, so Erez had become more authoritative toward everyone.

No one liked it.

She opened, "Hi, Uncle Erez. Come in."

"Hello Nava, my, you have grown since I have seen you. I saw your betrothed yesterday. He is a righteous young man, and I am happy for you."

"Thank you, Uncle."

Erez walked in past Nava. He carried his shepherd's staff in his hand. Erez was very tall, much taller than her father, Amos. He wore a long tunic that was too short for him and exposed his thin shins and ankles. He also had a narrow face and narrow jaw that was covered by a narrow black beard. Nava felt it fit his mean demeanor perfectly.

"Where is your father?" he asked in a stern tone.

"My mother went to fetch him from the backfield. He will be right back."

"Okay," Erez said as he sat down and tapped his foot.

"May I pour you a drink of cool water? I retrieved it from the well a little while ago," Nava asked.

"Yes, please."

Before Nava could finish, her Mother and Father entered the back door. "Erez!" her father Amos called as he removed his mantle and shook Erez's hand.

Amos asked, "To what do I owe this pleasure?"

"Good evening, brother. I need your help. One of my field hands has fallen ill. We need help for a few days bringing in the final harvest."

"Sure, I can help," Amos said. "But not until the day after tomorrow. I am helping Nava's betrothed, Aaron, and his father and brother rebuild a well on their land."

"I am helping, too," Nava said.

Amos turned, "We haven't decided if you will help yet, Nava. You know your mother needs you to help her and the other women with weaving tomorrow."

"I don't want to do weaving. I want to help build the well."

Erez laughed, "Working on a well is man's work, Nava, not woman's work."

"I am strong," Nava said.

Erez replied, "Not as strong as men, and it is men who do that kind of work." The way he said it, Nava knew it was meant to bring an end to the conversation.

"I can wield a sword; why can't I help build a well," Nava said.

"Sword?" Erez turned to Amos and Rebecca. "Your daughter is spending time learning how to use a sword?"

"What are you talking about?" Amos asked, turning to Nava.

"Aaron has taught me how to use a sword. We have been practicing for the last..."

Uncle Erez interrupted. "Nava, it is not bad that you are learning, but there is a difference between friendly learning and a real battle. A woman may learn to play with a sword, but she would surely die in a real battle against a man. That is why women have different things to do."

"Enough of all this silly talk," Rebecca said. "Nava, come with me. I need your help in the courtyard. And... I will need you tomorrow for our weaving, too. One of the women cannot make it. You will have to help us."

"But Mama, I already told Aaron I was coming!"

"Nava?" Amos said, motioning with his eyes for her to acquiesce."

Nava frowned and lowered her head. She felt humiliated, and worse than that, she felt put down. Aaron would never treat her like this, and she longed for the day they would marry and start their own home.

~ ~ ~ ~

The next day, a voice within her was urging her to go to the well. She asked her parents again, but they insisted she stay home with the women to assist with the weaving. So, she did, dutifully doing what was expected of her.

~ ~ ~ ~

Around two o'clock, the weaving was nearly finished, and most of the women had left. There was a pounding at the door, and a frantic voice yelled, "Nava! Come quickly. Something has happened to Aaron."

Nava's head turned, and she looked from her kitchen table out the window. It was her friend, Leah, anxiously waving for her to come. *Something happened to Aaron? What is she...?* Nava's heart quickened as she threw on the wet tunic hanging on the clothesline that ran along the side of the house to the front. "What is it?" she cried, "What has happened?"

"There's been an accident," shouted Leah, "We must hurry."

Leah took off, running ahead. Nava followed closely behind, her sandals carrying her through the dusty village road past the small white houses with thatched roofs that dotted the main road in the village of Bethlehem. Nava knew where they were heading. Her beloved Aaron was working on the well, and she was supposed to be there today.

Nava shouted ahead, "Wait!"

Leah stopped and waited for her to catch up.

Nava pleaded, exasperated, unwilling to wait, "Tell me what happened!"

"I don't know," Leah shouted, "I was told something happened to Aaron, and I was to come and get you at once."

"Oh, no," Nava said, and they took off running again.

Soon, they reached the outskirts of the village where his family's farm was located. Nava could see others running ahead of them on their way to see what had happened. She and Leah ran up the final stretch of the road that ascended up the hill. As they reached the top, they saw a group of 20 people gathered around the new well. She could instantly tell something was wrong. The round structure that had stood 4 feet tall was damaged. Half the large stones that made up the wall were missing, seemingly fallen into the hole.

Nava quickly scanned the group. She saw her Father, Amos, staring down, along with Aaron's Father and brothers. All were frantically pulling stones and casting them aside. Aaron was not among them; everyone was crowded nearer and nearer the well, trying to peer in. A terrible sinking feeling in the pit of her stomach stiffened her, and her breath was seized. She burst ahead of Leah and pressed into the group, shouting frantically, "Let us through!" and crying out, "Where is Aaron?"

Nava saw the people turn toward her. Sad looks on their faces seemed to worsen as they realized it was her. Most lowered their glance downward as they stepped aside to allow her to pass through and get closer.

Nava peered down at what they were all looking at. Her betrothed, Aaron, was lying at the bottom of the well with his body partially submerged in the water. Most of his body was covered with over 20 large stones that had fallen in from the top. Blood covered most of his head. His eyes and his face were frozen in the grip of death.

"Aaron!" she screamed, trying to climb over the remaining wall.

"No, Nava," yelled a man behind her, who quickly pushed through and grabbed her, pulling her back. He turned her around and embraced her tightly. It was her grandfather, Caleb.

"Let me go!" she yelled.

Caleb glanced over his shoulder to the bottom of the well, then squeezed her tighter as she tried to wrest herself free. He whispered into her ear, saying tenderly, "He is gone, Nava. Aaron is gone."

"No!" she cried, "No!"

But he only held her more firmly, "I'm sorry... I'm sorry."

"He can't be!" she cried, "We are to be married in the Spring!"

She again tried to tear herself free and enter the well, but Caleb would not let her go. Finally, she collapsed in his arms, weeping. Caleb walked her through the crowd, away from the well, keeping a firm hold on her. Once away, she fell to her knees, raising her hands and eyes to Heaven, crying, "Adonai, God of my fathers, please help us!"

Chapter 6

The Village of Sidon
In the Northern Region of Judea
Three Years Later

Nava opened her eyes and peered out frum under her blanket at the sun entering her upstairs bedroom window. Her parents, Amos and Rebecca, were in the kitchen talking. She sighed, anxious at the thought of facing another day. Even with the light breezes coming off the Mediterranean Sea, it would be another scorching day in Sidon.

The Harvest Season had been unusually hot for the last month, making the long days in the fields even longer and very tiresome. Soon, though, the Winter Season would come, and she would welcome it. Winter meant she could be alone and at home more, inside her room more. She did not enjoy any seasons except winter any longer. The Spring, summer, and harvest times only reminded her of the days when she and her beloved Aaron frolicked endlessly in Bethlehem's hills and streams.

After Aaron's death, she retreated into a dark shell. She and Aaron were deeply in love and on the verge of embarking on the joys and mysteries of marriage, but it had all been taken from her, from them.

Everyone had wanted her to "snap out of it" to "go on with life" to "meet someone new," but she couldn't. Aaron was the only person who understood her and who would allow her to be herself. She was the same for him, understanding and loving his frailties and strengths.

When a year had passed with no change in her condition, her mother, Rebecca, turned to her family for help. They, too, were shepherds, but to the north, many days journey from Bethlehem. It would be a new start for Nava. After some visits and conversations, Rebecca's Father, Amos, was offered lands and flocks in Sidon. It would mean that one day, he could even take over the vast herds completely. Though many would consider the opportunity a blessing, none of that mattered to Nava's parents. Their only concern was for her. They reluctantly accepted their new life and left Bethlehem, hoping it might give her a new start.

That was two years ago now, and little had changed.

~ ~ ~ ~

She closed her eyes again and tried to go back to sleep. But then she heard her mother speaking louder from the kitchen. "No, Amos, you must take her with you. She needs to go back."

"It is too dangerous, Rebecca," her father said gently but firmly. Nava loved him for this quality of being such a loving and kind leader in their home. He was the strongest man she ever knew, yet he was the kindest at the same time.

Her mother would not relent, whispering louder, "Amos, please trust me. She will waste away here. She is already 24 years old. I fear this dark spell will be with her forever. What if she never marries or never has children because of it?"

"Rebecca, please, don't say those things!"

"Amos, I feel strongly about this. You will be able to keep her safe on the journey. It is only six days. It will be good for her to see her cousins, aunts and uncles, and most of all, her beloved Grandfather, Caleb. I know she misses him."

There was quiet, and Nava now understood. They must be talking about going back to Bethlehem. She felt a shiver of fear run up her spine. To go back was to face what had happened to Aaron again. It would remind her of the day her life ended for good.

"I will think it over, Rebecca."

"Please, Amos. You must consider it."

Again, there was quiet, and Nava knew what this meant. Her Father was leaning toward her going. But when? For how long? And, more importantly, why? She laid awake for a long time, thinking about the day at the well so long ago when the falling boulders had killed Aaron. She curled up in a fetal position and silently wept until she fell back asleep.

Chapter 7

Nava's Father entered her room early in the morning the following day. "Good morning, Nava. I have news."

Nava sighed. She did not want to get out of bed today, and her depression was pressing on her mind heavily. She closed her eyes and asked, "What is the news?"

"Your Uncle Erez sent a messenger pigeon to us yesterday. Something is happening in Bethlehem, and your Grandfather Caleb wants us there. He said we should come right away."

Nava's eyes tightened further. She did not want to talk about this. "I don't want to go, Father."

"Oh, now, Nava, it will be a wonderful journey. Just you and I are going. It will be nice to spend time together."

"I don't want to go back there, Father. And... I don't like Uncle Erez."

Amos chuckled, "I understand. Many of us don't like Uncle Erez either. He is the oldest, though, and now that your grandfather is so feeble, Uncle Erez is the Patriarch of our family."

Nava opened her eyes wide, "He is mean, Father. You should be the Patriarch."

The smile on Amos's face fell away some, "You know, Nava, that the oldest male is the one to become the Patriarch. I know Uncle Erez can be mean, but he is my brother and has good qualities, too. "

She closed her eyes tightly again, "Father, I am afraid."

Her Father did not reply, and she knew he was thinking. She kept her eyes shut, waiting, then felt his strong hand gently rub her upper arm. He softly brushed her hair away from her face, saying. "It will be okay. It will be good for you."

Nava exhaled the last remnants of her attempt at resistance. She asked, "When are we leaving?"

"Tomorrow morning."

She turned over and curled up under the blanket.

~ ~ ~ ~

The next morning, Nava came out of the house carrying some of her clothing, neatly wrapped in a bundle. Her Father and mother stood beside their wooden cart attached to their two donkeys, Sasha and Sid. They would need both donkeys to ensure no trouble on the six-day journey. Should any misfortune come to one of the animals, the other could pull them the rest of the way.

Rebecca took the bundle from her, put it in the cart, and hugged her tightly. "Oh, my precious daughter, may our God be with you and protect you on your journey."

"Thank you, Mama. I will be back before you know it." Even as the words left Nava's mouth, she realized it could be the last time she would see her mother. She hugged her tighter, saying, "I am sorry I have disappointed you."

"You have not disappointed me. You are my beautiful flower and a daughter of Israel. I love you, Nava. Don't worry. God will help you."

"Thank you," Nava said, wiping a tear from her eye. She half-smiled and got into the seat of the cart. Amos loaded a few more pouches and then went back inside the house. He emerged moments later carrying his sword and dagger and carefully placed them in the cart to reach them if needed. He kissed his wife once more, then got in next to Nava.

"Wait," Nava cried. She jumped down from the cart and ran into the house. Moments later, she ran out carrying the sword Claudius had given Aaron. She had retrieved it from the cave after his death.

"What are you doing?" Rebecca exclaimed.

"I am bringing Aaron's sword with me."

Her mother protested, "Amos, tell her no."

Amos agreed, "Nava, you don't need the sword. Leave it here."

"No, Father. Aaron taught me how to use it." Seeing her mother's face grow more alarmed by the moment, she made an excuse, "Mother, I want to give it back to Aaron's family when we get to Bethlehem."

Rebecca's face relaxed, and she looked at Amos.

Amos said, "Alright, but wrap it up in a cloth. I don't want you getting hurt."

Nava lifted it, brandished it, and smiled, "I know how to handle it, Father, but I will do as you say." She pulled out a cloth, wrapped her sword, and tucked it away.

Moments later, Amos pulled on the reins and yelled, "Hah," signaling for Sasha and Sid to start down the road. Nava turned one more time, waving goodbye to her mother. She turned again before they crested a hill, watching her mother and her home fade into the distance.

Chapter 8

Within the hour, Nava was transported to a serene and captivating landscape into the heart of Judea's countryside. The arid terrain felt alive with a timeless beauty that had witnessed countless generations pass along it.

The winding road through the gently rolling hills adorned with sparse patches of wildflowers painted the landscape with bursts of color as if nature sought to contrast the earthy tones of the soil and rocks.

After a while, Nava nudged her father and pointed to the distance, where a group of shepherds were tending to their flocks. "Look, father, they must live nearby." He nodded, appreciating the serene beauty of the ride as much as her. Occasionally, a goat or two could be seen perched on rocky outcroppings, using their remarkable agility to navigate the rugged terrain.

It all felt so wonderful. But Nava's excitement began to wear off by the middle of the first day. The depression she had endured for years, with all its daily fears and daily worries, came roaring back. It pained her to sit on the cart's bench, trudging along so slowly. "Father," she asked, "Can I lie down in the back of the cart? I am very tired."

Amos called out, "Whoa," pulling Sasha and Sid to a stop. "Are you okay, Nava?" he asked tenderly.

"No, I don't feel very well. I want to lay down."

"Sure," he said as he hopped down from the cart seat and went around to the back to make room and position some blankets and clothing to make it comfortable for her.

Once he was finished, she climbed into the back, covered her face with her headdress, and closed her eyes. Amos started again but went more slowly to minimize the noise and bumps.

The rest of the day felt long and hot on the road, but they made satisfactory progress and did not experience any problems. When evening descended, Amos pulled off the road and went down into a small valley where they could not be seen from the road. He set up a small camp and lit a fire to cook some of the lentils his wife had packed for them. He set Nava up with a log to sit on to stir them until they were cooked. When they were ready, they allowed them to cool, then enjoyed the meal with some small pieces of bread.

She did not say much during the meal. She felt as down as she ever had and knew her father understood. He did not press her nor try to 'get her to snap out of it.' Somehow, he understood she needed time, and she loved him for this. Once it began to grow dark, they extinguished the fire, and they bedded down near it with the cart and the donkeys tied up not far away.

The following day, they got an early start, and Nava felt better by the time the sun had risen. They were in the hill country now, with all its luster and beauty. Endless small trees and flowers scattered among patches of grass that cascaded up and down endless hills. As they went up and down the hills, following the road used by travelers for centuries, the rising sun appeared, bringing warmth to her face. She felt hope for the first time in a very long time. Hope for what, she was not sure, but hope, nonetheless.

Chapter 9

Midway through the day, Nava asked her father, "Father, why did Uncle Erez insist we come right away? What could be so important?"

"Uncle Erez did not say, but your grandfather, Caleb, urged us to come immediately. He also specifically asked that you come too."

"Oh, I miss Grandfather," Nava said dreamily, "I can't wait to see him. Is he well?"

"He has grown old and feeble, Nava. He can no longer work in the fields with the other shepherds, but from what I hear, he goes out with them anyway."

"I love him. I have forgotten how much over the last few years."

Nava wondered about this. The years of depression had taken so much from her. She had forgotten about many things and many people. Suddenly, her friend Leah came to mind. Her brave and beautiful friend. They had grown up together, and Leah introduced her to Aaron shortly after his family moved to the outskirts of Bethlehem. Leah was so much what Nava wanted to be: tall, with dark piercing eyes and long flowing black hair. She was outgoing, talkative, and funny. Nava had long realized that were it not for Leah, she may never have spent enough time with Aaron to fall in love. Leah always organized their small group of friends to meet and do fun things together. It was Leah who pulled her along in life.

"Father, I forgot about Leah. How is she?"

"I heard she is well but have not heard more."

"How could I have forgotten about her?"

Amos replied, "It's okay, Nava. Sometimes, when something terrible happens, we block out many things."

Nava shook her head, upset that she had let this happen. She asked, "Has she married yet?"

Amos paused, and Nava saw he was contemplating what to tell her. He said, "I don't know, Nava, but I believe she still lives in Bethlehem. You will see her soon."

Nava felt joy and then a sinking feeling of shame. She was 24 and would soon be considered too old to marry. She closed her eyes, grimacing in the recesses of her mind. It was her fault. She should have found someone else after Aaron died. Instead, she shrunk under the blankets of her room and went into a dark hole. Leah would be ashamed of her or, worse, pity her.

Nava's countenance remained low as they lumbered along, up and down the dirt road as it rose and fell amongst the hills of the hill country. Hours and hours passed slowly.

Chapter 10

Later in the day, they heard a woman scream when the sun was on its descent. Amos shouted, "Whoa," pulling the cart to a stop. He leaped off, saying, "Stay here, Nava."

The scream came again. It was beyond the nearby hill. Nava watched her father grab his sword and dagger. He ran quietly to the top of the hill, then ducked down and crawled to the crest.

Nava jumped out of the cart and went after him, crawling up behind him. He turned, "Nava, I told you to stay in the cart."

"What is happening?"

"Keep your head down. Someone is being robbed."

Nava peered up slightly. A family of four was kneeling below them on the other side of the hill. Standing before them were four men dressed in different colored tunics and all wearing sandals. Their heads were covered, wrapped tightly around their faces to hide their identities. They all held swords and were rummaging through the family's belongings, tossing the contents of their bags and bundles all over the desert sand.

"What should we do, Father?" Nava asked anxiously.

Amos said nothing but was in deep thought. Finally, he subtly shook his head, "We cannot help them, Nava. There are too many of them."

Nava nodded, relieved. She had thought about returning to the cart to get Aaron's sword but was very afraid.

She and her father crept back down a few yards, then got up and ran to their cart. Amos took the bridle of Sasha and Sid and slowly led them down the road, moving away from the family.

After a while, they returned to the cart seat and continued their journey faster. Nava asked, "Father, should we have helped them?"

He shook his head, "There was nothing we could do. Those men were not going to hurt them. They were only going to rob them. Had we tried to intervene, it may have turned violent."

Nava nodded, but for the rest of the day, she wondered if there was something they could have done. Would not she and her father have made formidable foes against those bandits?

She imagined they would have.

Chapter 11

On the fourth day of their journey, they found themselves on a long stretch of the road, which seemed particularly desolate. It was a flatter part of the hill country, with fewer trees and hills. This made Amos nervous, as hills and trees provided natural shelter from the eyes of other distant travelers and, more importantly, from the eyes of distant bandits.

When night came, Nava and her father lit the fire, talked for a while over dinner, and then bedded down for the night, and soon they were fast asleep. During the night, after the fire had dipped low, Nava felt a blade on her throat and heard a gruff voice say, "Get up, woman, and keep silent, or I will kill you."

She shuddered and sat up slowly.

Across the way, on the other side of the fire, another man dressed in black garb and wearing a black turban held a dagger to her father's side.

"Father!" Nava called. The man holding the knife to her neck slapped her on the head, "Silence, woman."

"Keep quiet, Nava," her father shouted sternly. He glanced at the man behind him, holding the dagger into his side, and said, "You may take our money. It is in that pouch under the seat of the cart."

"Shut up," the man replied, jabbing the dagger more forcefully, puncturing Amos's skin. "We will take whatever we want."

The man with Nava took his dagger and quickly slit the top-fastening string of her tunic. The top of her tunic fell partially open. She clenched her arms tightly around her chest, holding it up.

The man nervously laughed and said defiantly, "Perhaps we will take our fill of her."

Suddenly, Amos thrust his elbow up into the face of the man in the black garb. Then, in one swift action, Amos tumbled forward and rolled, picking up his sword from the ground where he slept. He crouched, facing the man in the black garb. The man with Nava shoved her aside and moved forward to engage Amos.

Amos yelled, "Nava, run!"

Nava bolted into the darkness, but just far enough to watch. Amos did not wait for the other attacker but leaped toward the man in the black garb. He thrust his sword downward with more force than she thought he was capable of, slashing deeply into the shoulder of the man. The man screamed as his arm, nearly severed, dangled unnaturally. He waved his dagger recklessly and fell to the side, incapacitated.

But Amos never saw the other man coming. The other man leaped on him, knocking him to the ground. He was much larger, and in a moment, he had him pinned to the ground, with his dagger raised into the air, trying to drive it down into Amos's chest. Only Amos's tight grip on the man's wrist was stopping him.

Nava ran to the cart. She unwrapped Aaron's sword and ran around the cart. The man's back was to her, and he held the dagger high, only Amos's strong grip stopping the thief from plunging it down. She stepped forward three steps. A voice within knew what she needed to do. But Uncle Erez's critical words played, too, "When a woman fights a man, she will die."

Her hand began to shake, and her knees trembled. Suddenly, Amos lost his grip, and the man drove the dagger downward into his shoulder. Amos yelled out in horrific pain. The man was on top of him now and began to choke him.

Nava gritted her teeth. There was still time; she tried to lift the sword; she only needed to plunge, but she was frozen in fear. Suddenly, her father gave a tremendous shout and pulled his dagger out of his belt, thrusting it deeply under the man's ribs.

The man screamed and fell off to the side. He rolled over and scampered up, picked up his wounded friend, and they both raced into the desert darkness.

Nava watched him go, then ran to her father, falling to her knees beside him. The long dagger was buried deep within his shoulder, coming out the back and pinning him to the ground.

"Father! Father! Are you okay?" she cried through tear-stricken eyes.

~ ~ ~ ~

Amos's head bobbed in pain. His breathing was labored. He said, "Nava... go... go... get a stick from the fire."

"Why, Father?"

"Just do it... hurry. It must be red hot!"

She ran to the fire and picked up a stick jutting out on one end while the other was bright orange, glowing with heat. She brought it over and knelt beside him, worried about what he would do.

He labored to breathe and glanced up, "Nava, listen very carefully; you must be brave, or I may die. You have to pull the dagger out, then shove the hot end of the stick into my wound. Put it in…. and hold it for three seconds. Then, you must help me to turn my body over very quickly. You must run to the fire, get another stick, and do the same thing to the wound in the back. Do you understand?"

"No, Father, I cannot do that to you."

"Nava, listen to me! You must do exactly as I said. I will scream in pain now, but you must not let that stop you. You must do this. Do you understand?"

She closed her eyes tightly, "Oh, Father, I don't know… if…"

"Nava, you must! Or I will die…" his voice trailed off, and he winced in pain.

"Okay, okay," she said, opening her eyes and moving closer, holding the stick in one hand. She felt like fainting, like running away and hiding. This was too much for her.

Amos looked up, "First, get another stick. It must be right out of the fire."

Nava hurled the stick in her hand into the desert night and ran to the fire. She got one out and readied another for retrieval after she turned him over. She ran over and nervously uttered, "I am ready, Father."

"Place your hand on the dagger handle and pull. Then, shove the red-hot stick in firmly. Now! Do it!"

She reached down, grabbed the dagger, and pulled it out. "*Ahh!*" he yelled.

She threw it aside, took the stick, placed the glowing ember side into the wound, and then pressed it in.

"*Ahhhhh!*" he screamed.

Nava began to cry as she pulled it up.

"Turn me over… quickly!" Amos shouted.

She labored to help him roll over, then ran to the fire. She took the freshly glowing stick out of the fire and placed it into the wound on his back. She cringed at the sickening sound and smell of burning flesh.

"*Ahhh!*" he screamed again, louder this time. In the next moment, his face fell to the side, unconscious.

Nava sighed heavily and began to shudder. She closed her eyes, gathering her courage, trying to push down the trauma within her. She got up and covered her father with a blanket. Then, she knelt next to him and examined the wound. It was too dark. She retrieved a stick with a flame from the fire and held it to the wound. Now she could see. It had stopped bleeding. Whatever her father had told her to do seemed to have worked. She had done it.

She looked around in the darkness surrounding them. It scared her to know she was alone. Her father was with her, and yet, she was alone. She got her blanket and curled up next to him, and after a long time of praying and worrying, she finally fell asleep.

Chapter 12

The following day, Nava dreamily heard the sound of birds chirping their morning song. She opened her eyes and looked over at her father. He was still unconscious, but something was different. He looked pale, and he was sweating.

She ran to the cart and got a rag, then took a jar and emptied some water on it. She knelt next to him and gently wiped the sweat from his face. He did not wake but only moaned. She wished her mother was there to help and guide her, but her mother was miles and miles away.

She wiped his brow with a damp cloth for several hours, trying to wake him gently, but he would wake up fully. She knew there was no way she could lift him into the cart. Until he woke up, they were stuck.

After the sun had passed the high noon mark, he finally woke.

"Father, are you all right?"

He looked at her and nodded. He was pale, whiter than she had ever seen, with beads of sweat formed on his forehead and upper cheeks. His eyes were sunken and half-closed.

"Can you make it into the cart?"

Amos glanced over at the cart and sighed, then nodded slowly. "Bring it closer," he said in a feeble voice.

Nava took the cart and turned it around, maneuvering it back toward him. She put some sticks in front of the wheels so the cart would not move. He held onto her while he pulled himself up to a sitting position, wincing in pain as he did. Nava then helped him to stand. He cried out in pain, then limped to the back of the cart and fell backward into it, wincing. But he was in.

Nava helped him arrange his legs, prepared a makeshift pillow, and covered him with a blanket. Next, she gathered up the camp and hitched Sasha and Sid to the cart. She decided she would take her Father and return to their home. She climbed into the cart seat and headed in the other direction, back toward home.

"Wait!" her father moaned, "Where... are... you going?"

"I am taking you home, Father."

He lifted his head, "No, Nava. We must go to... Bethlehem. We are closer to Bethlehem than to home."

Nava stopped. She feared going to Bethlehem, especially with her father so weak. What might await them there? What might her Uncle Erez demand she and her father do? What if he died? She would be all alone. He was right, though. They were closer.

"I will turn back to Bethlehem. Go to sleep now." She turned Sasha and Sid around and headed for Bethlehem.

The day on the dusty road was long and lonely. They saw only a few travelers coming in the other direction, and Nava would not engage them. She trusted no one.

As night drew near, she began to feel nervous. She would now have to set up camp and start a fire independently. If trouble came, it would be up to her to repel it. She began scouting ahead for a place to stop and hide out for the night.

She kept going down the road until they came to a place where she felt they would be somewhat hidden from the road, then pulled off. She made a camp, started a fire, then helped her father down and propped him up on the ground near the fire. She got them some bread and warmed up some dried fish her mother, Rebecca, had wisely packed for them.

Her Father fell asleep, and Nava lay beside him, with Aaron's sword tucked next to her body. Should anyone attack them tonight, she would be ready. She could not sleep for a long time, worried that her father was weakening, but finally, she fell asleep.

During the night, her father began to moan. Nava woke and knelt beside him, "Father, what is wrong?" But he only moaned louder. She noticed his head was covered with sweat and felt his forehead. He was burning up with a fever. She ran to the cart, got the jar of water, and brought it closer to them. She dampened a rag, wiped his face, covered him with blankets, and put more wood on the fire. After a while, he fell back asleep, and she, too, went back to sleep.

An hour later, his moaning continued. It was still very dark, but she needed help, and though her father was in no shape to travel, they would have a better chance of finding help on the road. In the dead of night, she packed up the camp and helped her father onto the cart. Then, slowly, she headed along the road in the darkness, up and down the hills, toward Bethlehem. It was hard at first to see the road, but before long, her eyes adjusted, and the moon rose in the sky, allowing her to keep moving ahead. She needed to sleep, but there was no time.

Chapter 13

She thought they might only be two days away but was very unsure.

It didn't matter now.

It was the middle of the night, and time passed slowly. Suddenly, a voice rang out, "Halt!"

She immediately pulled Sasha and Sid to a stop and looked around. Two men ran over, holding spears and torches, with two others following closely behind them. They were dressed like soldiers, tall and strong, with stern faces. The leader yelled, "Who are you?"

Nava nervously replied, shaking, "I am traveling to Bethlehem. Bandits have wounded my father." She pointed to the back of the cart.

One of the men held his torch over Amos. He was unconscious, with his eyes barely open. His tunic was badly stained with blood on the shoulder area.

The leader said, "Search them for weapons."

At once, they pulled Nava from the cart seat. Two of the men searched her. They picked up Aaron's weapon from under the cart seat. Nava protested, "Please, that sword is important to me."

The leader examined it and said, "I will keep it for now."

The other two searched her father, taking his sword and dagger.

When they were satisfied, the leader said, "Follow us."

"Where are you taking us?" Nava exclaimed in a frightful tone.

"Just follow us, and all will be well."

Nava nervously returned to the cart and pulled on the reins, steering Sasha and Sid forward. They followed the four men off the road, down a hillside, and around another hill. Soon, they entered a clearing set in the middle of several hills. There were over 30 camels and several oxen, with several fires lit and numerous large tents set up. Nava counted at least ten men like them, standing guard, all dressed in the same uniforms, with light breastplates and thin helmets. Each carried a sword on a belt around his waist and a spear in his hand. Each looked alert, peering into the darkness for signs of trouble. One tent was by far the largest of them all. Lamps were lit inside, sending a glow across the entire camp. Nava wondered why she had not seen them and marveled that they were hidden well. The men pulled her cart into the clearing and helped her dismount.

Chapter 14

"Wait here," the leader said as he set down his spear and went into the largest tent.

Moments later, he came out. "They will see you now."

"Who?" Nava asked, afraid. "Our leaders. They are wealthy merchants."

"But what of my Father?" she asked frightenedly.

"Don't worry. One of my men will stay with him. He is too sick to move." He pointed, "Go inside."

Nava hesitated for a moment, then stepped toward the tent's entrance. She pulled back the flap and stepped inside. Her feet immediately felt the plush carpet that stretched before her. Tall lamps were lit at another entryway to what seemed like an inner chamber to the vast tent. Inside, six more men stood guard. while others were milling about nervously beyond them. Silence hung in the quiet air, laced with tension and nerves, and Nava was too scared to make a sound.

She continued forward and pulled back the second flap. Several people paused to glance at her. Most were standing, but three men were sitting in a semi-circle in the center of the room.

One wore a blue robe and a matching blue turban on his head. He bowed and said, "I am Casal. Greetings to you. What is your name?"

"My name is Nava."

The other man next to him was a dark-skinned man. His robe was maroon and gold and seemed very large on him. His head was wrapped in a gold-colored turban. He said, "My name is Azar. What happened to you and your father?"

Nava nodded in greeting, then said, "Two men attacked us. They…" She lowered her head, "They were going to rape me, but my father stopped them."

The third man lowered his eyes, shaking his head. He wore a black silk robe and a white silk cloth covering his neck and chest. A black and gold turban covered his head. He said, "My name is Malchia. Don't worry. We will help your father."

Malchia raised his finger and turned his head toward the side of the tent, calling out, "Farad."

A strikingly handsome young man who looked to be near her age bowed and hustled forward. His skin was very tan, and his eyes were dark, complementing his dark black hair. He wore a red turban and a long tan tunic tied at the waist with a red cloth. His ankles and calves were wrapped tightly in the same red cloth, and on his feet were brown sandals. He was the most elaborate and impressive-looking servant Nava had ever seen.

He stood beside Nava and faced the three men, bowing, "Yes, my Lords."

Malchia said, "Nava, this is my chief steward, Farad. He will care for you and your father's needs while you are with us."

"But we cannot stay," she replied abruptly.

The merchant named Azar said, "We have been told your Father is gravely ill. He will need our help if he is to recover."

Nava exhaled loudly, realizing that God was helping her through these men. She nodded, saying, "Thank you."

Malchia nodded, and Farad bowed and left the tent to attend to her father.

Nava was unsure if she should go with him. She started following him when the merchant Malchia called, "Where are you traveling to?"

"To Bethlehem," Nava replied. She looked up, realizing she did not even know where she was. She asked, "Where are we now?"

Azar replied, "We are not far from the village of Nazareth, a two-day journey to Jerusalem. "

Nava nodded. She had thought they were two days out.

Azar asked, "Why are you going to Bethlehem?"

Nava felt uneasy for a moment. Why would these men be interested in such a tiny village as Bethlehem? Were they foreign invaders? Did they wish the people of Bethlehem harm? How could they? They had only a few men with them.

She replied, "I used to live in Bethlehem. My Grandfather wrote to us and told us to come at once. He said something important was happening there and wanted my father and I to see it."

The men considered her answer.

She asked, "Where are you going?"

Malchia said, "We have business near Jerusalem, the same route you are traveling. You may travel with us for the next few days. It will be safer for you."

He turned to the others, "How fitting that a young woman of Israel would be with us for the last part of our journey." Then, he turned to Nava, "In the morning, when your father is ready, we will leave. We have a few more days journey until we arrive."

Nava bowed slightly and said, "Thank you."

Chapter 15

The following morning, Nava was awakened by a great commotion outside her tent. She looked over at her father, peacefully asleep on a plush pillow and covered with the warm blanket that Farad had given to them. She got up and went to the tent's entrance to see what was happening. She opened the flap and stepped outside.

Men were taking tents down, packing them up, and loading them onto loud camels, protesting the burdens they would carry. Other men were going in all directions, breaking down the camp. Farad was giving orders to all, and Nava realized that he was in charge, though he looked to be the youngest. When he spoke, men moved, and many turned to him with questions. The merchants were alone in the distance, on top of a hill, looking toward the direction of the road they would soon be taking. Farad saw her, and he came right over.

He bowed, "Good morning, young lady. Did you sleep well?"

"Yes, I did, thank you."

"Your Father is improving. I checked in on him during the night. We will get him into your cart and pack your tent soon. I will be traveling with you in the cart."

Nava looked momentarily alarmed, "I don't know if Sasha and Sid can handle it."

Farad turned his head slightly, asking, "Who are Sasha and Sid?"

"They are my donkeys."

Farad chuckled, "Oh, don't worry. One of our oxen is going to pull the cart. It will go smoother. Sasha and Sid will be tied up behind us and follow along."

"Oh, okay. Thank you."

Farad smiled at her, and Nava felt a warmth she had not felt since the marvelous days she had spent with Aaron. It surprised her, as she had forgotten how wonderful it felt for a man to notice her. She went to her tent to wake her father and gather her things for the journey.

Finally, the camels were lined up, and the merchants mounted their camels. Farad walked up and down the long line of men, beasts, and carts. At the very end of the line was Nava in her cart. A large ox, one of the largest she had ever seen, was before her, hitched to the cart. Farad went to the front of the line and waved everyone forward, watching them go, doing a final inspection of all the supplies as they passed by him. When Nava came near, he jumped up on the cart and sat beside her. He took the reins and shouted a command in a language Nava did not understand. "What did you say?" she asked.

"I told him to stop being lazy."

Nava laughed and laughed. She was so happy that Farad and his band had found them, and she wondered about this dashing man who sat next to her.

As the day wore on, she and Farad talked about their countries. Nava told him all about Bethlehem. She told him of her people's struggle, especially with the Romans, and of the hope that some held that a Messiah would come.

"Do you believe there will be a Messiah?" Farad asked.

She did not want to seem foolish, so she said, "I am not sure; I mean, people have believed it for hundreds of years. It seems, well, maybe, that God has forgotten us."

"What do you think?" Farad asked.

Nava was quiet momentarily, then she smiled, "I believe it. Only because not believing it leaves me with no hope at all."

"No hope?"

She wiped a tear from her eye. The loss of Aaron had stolen all of her hope. "I was betrothed once, and he was killed. I lost my hope for living on that day."

"When was that?"

She hesitated, unable to talk about it, but said, "Around three years ago."

"Hmmm," Farad said. He glanced at her and said, "I admire you, Nava."

"Oh, why is that?"

"You have a dignity about you, a goodness. I can tell by the way you spoke to my masters and how you speak about your family. You honor the old ways, don't you."

She blushed. She did not know he was watching her, but she was glad. It felt good to be noticed by a young man. It had been so very long.

There was silence for several minutes, and Nava was unsure what to say. She felt uncomfortable, as if talking with another young man betrayed her beloved Aaron.

Farad broke the silence, "Nava, do you see that tall man on the camel with the black spear?"

She looked ahead in the caravan of men and beasts. The man Farad spoke of was about six camels ahead of them. "Yes, I see him."

Farad looked at her, shaking his head.

"What is it?" she asked.

"That man is from Babylon. He snores so loud you would fall over if you heard him. Did you hear him last night?"

Nava laughed, "No, I did not."

Farad's eyes widened as he exclaimed, "Well, the camels did. He woke them in the middle of the night with the loudest snore I ever heard. I had to go into his tent and tell him to be quiet."

Nava laughed loudly. She hit him in the arm playfully, saying, "You are exaggerating."

"Oh, no, I am not. There are some strange men in our group. Look, do you see that round one, up ahead, let's see, on the eighth camel in front of us."

Nava looked, standing for a moment, then sitting back down. "Yes, I see him."

Farad looked at her again, shaking his head, "That man is from the city of Ur. He eats more food than any person I have ever seen in my life. He could eat an entire ox if he were allowed."

Nava laughed again. "You are joking!"

"Oh, no, I am not! I just hope we get to Jerusalem soon because we are running out of food. We either have to get more food, or we have to get rid of him. I have not decided which is the best solution yet. But I will."

Nava hit him on the shoulder again, "Stop kidding me."

"Oh, there is no kidding going on here, Nava. We are with wealthy merchants and three groups of men, all Persians, yes, but some are very different. You will see."

Nava smiled and settled into a time of quiet reflection as they road up and down through the hill country. They were nearing Bethlehem, she could tell. There were more trees and much more green grass. Soon, she would return to the city where her beloved had died.

She looked over at Farad. She loved his animated stories that made her laugh. She realized it had been long since she laughed… not since Aaron.

Chapter 16

They reached a higher elevation plateau and set up camp for the night. The sun was just beginning to head toward the distant horizon. It would give time for tents to be struck, fires to be lit, and food to be cooked.

The place buzzed with excitement and the noise of camels being unloaded and oxen groaning loudly as they were taken to a nearby stream to drink. Men were shouting, following the orders of Farad, who took charge of the decisions of who and what was to go where and ordered men to be about the needed tasks.

Nava set the reins down and peeked at her father. He was still asleep from the herbs he had been given before their setting out. She exited the cart and watched Farad racing about, firmly in command of the entire setup.

Before long, meals were served, dusk darkened, and the men gathered around the fires, sharing stories. Nava sat with Farad. Her father was already asleep in the tent. He had woken long enough to eat, but Nava encouraged him to go back to sleep, as he was indeed healing, and she did not want to hamper the process. Sitting around a fire was no place for a wounded man.

As Nava and Farad quietly watched the fire, the three leaders exited their tent and walked to the highest place on the plateau. One carried some instrument, and they gathered, and all looked to the southern sky.

"What are they doing?" Nava asked Farad.

"They are very interested in a star they have been following."

"Star, what star?"

"Come with me. We can speak to them."

Farad got up and helped Nava to stand. They walked across the camp to where the three leaders were.

"Azar, can you tell Nava about the star you have been watching."

They all turned, and Azar raised his hand, signaling them to come closer. Farad said, "Speak with them, Nava. I will see to your father."

The one called Malchia turned toward Nava. He was tall and carried himself with a presence few men possess. His arms rose gently within his flowing black silk robe as he pointed to the southern sky.

Malchia said, "Do you see that star, Nava?"

Nava looked, and though she had never noticed it, it was suddenly the largest star in the sky. "It's so beautiful," she said. "I've never noticed it. Does it have special meaning?"

Azar said, "My calculations show it is south of Jerusalem."

"I can't believe it. I've never seen anything like it." Nava said. She had never seen such a beautiful star in her life. It was magnificent, with long rays of light shining straight up and down through it and across it from right to left. Nava had the thought that it was trying to shine its light across the entire world, North and South, East and West.

She added, "Maybe that is why my grandfather told me to come immediately. Maybe he sees it too."

"There is where we are going, Nava."

"I thought you were going to Jerusalem?" she asked.

"We thought so too, but we follow that star. We first saw it over a year ago. Our calculations told us it would settle over Jerusalem. We have been traveling for over a month. Now that we are close, it appears to be settling far south of Jerusalem."

Azar said to the others, as if Nava was not there, "But perhaps it will move back toward Jerusalem. It must, as it would not merely settle in the middle of nowhere."

She looked back at Malchia with her mouth still open. He was smiling at her, and she understood he was pleased that she was in awe. She asked, "But why is that star so important?"

"Are you familiar with the sacred texts, Nava?"

"Yes, I am. All the men and women of Israel are."

"Then you are familiar with the Holy Text of the Book of Numbers. In stanza 24, it says, 'I shall see him, but not now: I shall behold him, but not soon: there shall come a Star out of Jacob, and a Scepter shall rise out of Israel.'"

"Yes, I have heard that. It speaks of the coming Messiah," Nava said proudly.

Malchia looked at the star, "That is why we set off a month ago for Jerusalem. We want to see this newborn King of the Jews. We too believe the star is so significant and wondrous that this King will be the Messiah, the long-awaited Savior of Israel."

Nava looked back up at it, and suddenly she understood.

She turned to the men, and her eyes widened, "But wait, there is another scripture. "It says, 'But you… umm...'" She stopped and looked down, searching her mind to remember the passage. She looked up, "My father knows it by heart." She turned to the tent he was in and saw lamps burning, saying, "He will know."

She ran to the tent.

The men followed her into the tent, gliding in colorful gold-laden attire. They gently approached and stood over Nava and her father, listening.

Farad knelt beside her father, holding a wet cloth on his head and cleaning his wound. Nava asked, "Father, what is the ancient text from the Prophet Micah that foretells the Messiah will be born in Bethlehem?"

Amos opened his eyes slowly and saw the three merchants Nava had brought into his tent. His eyes widened, and he looked to Nava, who reassured him. Then, a faint smile crossed his face. He raised one finger feebly into the air and said in a weak voice, "But you, Bethlehem Ephrathah, though you are little among the thousands of Judah, yet out of you shall come forth to Me, the One to be Ruler in Israel, whose goings forth are from of old, from everlasting."

Malchia's eyes wandered toward his companions as he said, "The star is settled south of Jerusalem. Bethlehem is south of Jerusalem."

Their faces of Casal and Azar considered what he had said, neither of them able to hide their growing wonder and excitement.

Nava was so proud of her father.

Azar asked, "Why have we never heard of this Prophet, Micah?"

Nava replied, "The Sacred Text of the Prophet Micah was not written in Babylon, like the other texts. It was written here, in Israel."

"How do you know this?" Melchior asked.

"My Grandfather Caleb taught me much about the Sacred Texts."

Malchia replied, "Your Grandfather must know something about what we seek. He, too, must be favored."

"Favored?" Nava asked.

"Yes," Malchia said, "We are all favored. It seems we are among the few who have been called to see this great event."

Casal said, "The King of Kings is about to be born in Bethlehem, and we have been called to witness his birth."

Then Malchia said, "Nava, we want to tell you and your father who we really are. We are kings from Persia. My name is Melchior, this man beside me is Caspar, and our tall friend here is Balthazar. We could not tell you because we are traveling in secret."

"Kings? You are all kings?"

Caspar smiled, "We are not too bad to be around, are we?"

Nava laughed, "No, I just… Oh my." She glanced to her father, then bowed low. "I am so happy you helped us. My father would be… maybe dead. I don't know what to say."

"You have said enough, Nava. Tomorrow, we will head straight for Bethlehem together."

The kings all nodded toward Nava's father in a gesture of thanks, then went out and back to look at the star. Nava followed them and joined them at the hilltop. They all stood quietly, marveling at the star.

As she watched, Nava considered all that had been spoken. She lowered her glance, thinking. *The Messiah, now in Bethlehem.* Her grandfather had told her that people had talked of the coming Messiah for centuries. Still, in Nava's lifetime, the hope and talk had faded. Many said it was a fantasy by the leaders to give the people false hope. Besides, the Romans would never allow a king to come. And yet, her grandfather said something very important was happening, and here were these Kings, coming to see too. *Indeed, something extraordinary must be taking place.* She looked into the eyes of all of them and said, "I believe it is true."

Chapter 17

The next day, they broke camp and headed out as early as possible. Their plan was to stay far from the outskirts of Jerusalem and pass around it to go straight to Bethlehem.

After several hours of journeying and a brief break for lunch, the caravan of over 20 camels and several oxen crested a hill, and suddenly, Jerusalem was visible on the distant horizon. They all stopped, marveling at the famous city, albeit from a great distance.

Nava smiled and said to Farad, "It is a beautiful city, but it is a sad city too, Farad. Our history has been difficult."

Farad nodded, then jumped out of the cart and ran up to the front of the caravan. He was checking briefly on everyone and signaling for them to start again.

One man pointed and called to Farad. He ran over quickly. "What is it?" Farad asked.

"Look," said the man.

In the distance, a cloud of dust could be seen. There were at least fifteen riders, all on horseback. As they drew nearer, Farad could tell now that they were Roman soldiers coming from the direction of the road that led to Jerusalem.

Farad pulled on the reins and called out for everyone to stop. He handed them to Nava, "Take the reins. I have to go to the front."

Nava watched Farad run forward and stop to speak with the kings. It looked like they had decided to wait.

When the soldiers were near, they slowed. They were Roman soldiers, probably from the garrison of Jerusalem under King Herod's command. The commander was a tall, rugged Roman Centurion. He wore a silver helmet with silver steel flanges covering his cheeks, with curved four-inch-tall red bristles running front to back on top of his helmet. He raised his hand high, slowing his men to a stop 20 yards away. He then rode up alone.

The Centurion said, "Greetings to you, Kings of Persia, in the name of Herod, King of Judea."

Balthazar replied, "Greetings to you too. We did not know King Herod was aware we were here."

"Oh, King Herod has loyal subjects everywhere. Nothing happens in Judea without his notice."

Balthazar nodded, "What does King Herod ask of us?"

The Centurion smiled, "He would like you and your caravan to come to the Palace. He would like to host you for dinner tonight."

Nava walked up to Farad, tugged on his arm, whispered something, and then returned to her cart.

Farad listened, then said, "King Balthazar, may I have a word?"

"Certainly." Balthazar leaned over, and Farad whispered into his ear.

"Ah, yes," Balthazar said, sitting back up. He returned to the Centurion and said, "We will gladly accept King Herod's invitation. We have a girl and her father at the back of this caravan. We found them on the road. We would like them to be able to continue on their journey. They are not with our group."

The Centurion looked back at the cart, then kicked his horse and rode closer. He glanced down at Nava's father asleep in the back, with Nava seated, holding the reins of the oxen. He paused momentarily, glancing back toward Jerusalem in the distance, then said, "That will be fine."

"Very well," Balthazar said. "You may return. We will be at the palace before long."

The Centurion bowed once more, then pulled his horse around. He rode ahead of his men, who all turned and followed.

Balthazar turned to Farad, signaling for him to come close. He whispered, "Go with them to Bethlehem, Farad. We will see you there before long."

"My Lord," he said, "Be careful what you say to King Herod. Nava tells me that all the people greatly fear him."

Balthazar turned to glance at the soldiers in the distance, riding back toward the ancient city. "Herod knows much more than we think, but we will be cautious."

Chapter 18

Only four hours later, Farad, Nava, and Nava's father, Amos, still lying in the back of the cart, made their way up the hill on the road on the outskirts of Bethlehem. As they crested it, Nava looked over at the well where Aaron had perished years earlier. It was now fully built and functioning, as evidenced by the few people standing around it, filling their jugs. She recognized some of them but kept her headdress over her head, concealing her identity. She wanted to be alone in her thoughts right now, along with the memory of Aaron. She looked for a moment, remembering the fateful day, then turned her head straight and promised to put it out of her mind for good. She needed to move forward in life. Aaron was in God's hands now, and her being sad about it would not help him.

As this cleansing moment washed through her, she privately lamented she had sunken so low and wasted so many years. Coming on this trip, difficult as it had been, had been a wonderful time of change for her. She looked over at Farad's smiling face, holding the reins of the oxen next to her, and wondered if he, too, was to be part of this time of change. She liked him.

Soon, they were heading down the main road. They passed the house Nava and her family used to live in. Another family lived there now. Nava found herself wishing they had never left. They then came to the home of her Uncle Erez and his family. She stopped the cart and got out. She knocked on the door, but a strange man answered. "May I help you?"

"Yes, my Uncle Erez and his family live here. My grandfather, too."

"Oh, I am sorry. Erez and his family moved two years ago to the village of Hebron, I believe."

"Moved?" Nava said, confused.

"Oh, but Erez and Caleb are both here. They are up there, outside the village." The man pointed to the other end of the village, where the caves were located.

"Oh, okay. Thank you."

Nava was confused. *Why hadn't Uncle Erez told them he was moving? Maybe he did, and her parents did not think it important.* She glanced back to see he was still out and decided she would ask him later. She got into the cart and continued on to the other end of the village.

They rode up the winding road that led down through a valley, then onto a hillside where several caves were in the wall of a small cliff. Beyond the caves, Nava could see a field with some tents in it. Hundreds of sheep were milling around, and then she saw him, her grandfather, Caleb, sitting on a rock, smoking a pipe. "There he is!" she exclaimed to Farad. "My grandfather!"

As Farad guided the cart up the hill, Nava jumped off and ran the rest of the way, crying out, "Grandfather, Grandfather!"

With his pipe in his mouth, Caleb turned, took it out, and stood up as if disbelieving his eyes. "Nava!" he cried as he began waving. Nava ran to him and leaped into his arms, hugging him tightly. Tears ran down her face, "Oh, Grandfather, I missed you so much."

"My dear granddaughter, I have missed you too." He kissed her warmly on the cheek, then hugged her tightly, looking behind her. "Where is your father?"

"He is in the back of the cart, Grandfather. He was injured on the way here. Bandits attacked us."

"Attacked," Caleb said as he immediately went to the cart. He considered Farad, but only for a moment. He went to the back of the cart and saw Amos lying with his eyes partially closed. Farad jumped off the cart and stood beside Caleb, saying, "I have put herbs on for three days now. He has been improving. Some of the herbs I gave him are causing him to sleep."

"Who are you?" Caleb asked.

"I am Farad. I am the chief steward for King Balthazar. We rescued Nava and her father on the road, and they traveled with us. Outside Jerusalem, Herod's soldiers redirected the three Kings I was traveling with to go to his palace for a feast. King Balthazar bid me stay with Nava and her father to ensure they arrived here safely."

"Where will you go now?"

"I am to wait here. King Balthazar will be coming here within a few days."

"Then you will stay with us," Caleb said. "Here, help me get him over to that tent." Farad jumped back in the cart and maneuvered it closer to the tent. They woke Amos and helped him to walk in and helped him to lay down.

Chapter 19

As they were tending to Amos, Uncle Erez walked in with his shepherd's staff in hand. He wore a long dark brown tunic with dusty sandals on his feet. He was a tall, thin man with a thin black beard that Nava thought looked ugly. It did little to hide the look of anger he always seemed to carry. His voice was loud and authoritative and, as usual, stern. "Nava, what happened to your father?"

"We were attacked, Uncle Erez."

Erez looked at his brother lying on the ground, covered with a blanket. Amos opened his eyes, "Hello, Erez."

Erez smiled, "Hello, brother. Are you going to be okay?"

"Yes, this man is helping me."

Erez turned and looked at Farad suspiciously. "Who are you?" he asked.

"I am the steward of King Balthazar. Three Kings from the region of Persia will be here soon. They are coming to see the newborn King of the Jews."

Erez scoffed slightly, "That is what I am told, but I don't know what the Romans will have to say about a newborn King."

Caleb shook his head, "Forgive my son for not believing the message we were given."

"What message?" Nava asked.

Before Caleb could answer, Erez abruptly turned to leave, then stopped, turning to Farad. "You may stay in the camp with my men. I will see that you have what you need. Nava, you will stay in the tent with your father."

When Uncle Erez left, Nava could feel the tension leave and follow him out of the tent. She sighed. Uncle Erez had a way of making a person feel on edge. She had forgotten this about him. One never felt good once he was near, and it always took time for the uneasy feeling to disappear.

Her grandfather said, "Don't worry about him, Nava. I don't know why my son has become so bitter about life. It seems it gets worse as he grows old." Caleb noticed Amos had fallen back asleep. He put his finger to his lips, signaling quiet, and whispered, "Let's step outside."

They all walked outside the tent and stood in front of it. "Nava, Farad, listen while I tell you what happened."

Nava looked up with hopeful eyes, needing to cleanse herself of her uncle's demeanor.

Chapter 20

Caleb began, "One night, a little over a week ago, we were in our fields outside of Hebron. A bright light came over us in the sky, and an Angel from Heaven spoke to us."

Nava's mouth opened wide. "Are you sure, Grandfather?"

"Of course I am. I may be old, but I am not blind. One of our men was with me. You know him, Nathan."

"Yes, I remember him," Nava said.

"The Angel was right above us, Nava. She was a beautiful female Angel with long brown hair and deep blue eyes. I will never forget her face. It bore a profound peace and kindness I have rarely seen in a woman."

"Oh, Grandfather, you *are* favored."

Caleb nodded, "She said to us, 'Do not be afraid. I bring you good news that will cause great joy for all the people. Today, in the village of David, a Savior has been born to you; he is the Messiah, the Lord. This will be a sign to you: You will find a baby wrapped in swaddling clothes and lying in a manger.'" Caleb paused as a wide smile came over his face. He looked up into the sky as he probably had that night. His face seemed to glow.

He said, "Suddenly a great company of the heavenly Angels appeared, hundreds of them, praising God and singing in beautiful harmonious unison, 'Glory to God in the highest heaven, and on earth peace to those upon whom his favor rests.'"

Nava felt tears of happiness running down her cheeks. What her grandfather had just told her was the most beautiful thing she had ever heard. *Upon whom his favor rests.* She realized that he had been called, as the Kings had said, and that her grandfather was highly favored, and she realized she was highly favored, and her father, and Farad, all of them. They were all favored. It felt overwhelming.

Caleb noticed her and asked. "What is wrong, Nava?"

"Oh, Grandfather, I am so overwhelmed to hear all this. I have missed you so much. It's been so hard, Grandfather... these last years. It's just all so hard."

He rubbed her back, holding her tightly, "My dear girl, don't worry. Everything is going to be okay."

She looked up with a deep frown on her tear-stained face, "But I failed to protect Father. When the man was attacking him, I could have stopped him. I had my sword in my hand, Grandfather. I only had to use it. But I was afraid. I hesitated, and the man stabbed him."

"Nava, don't blame yourself. Women are givers of life, not takers of life. You did what any woman would do." He turned to Farad, "God sent you help. Do you not see that Farad is helping you?"

She wiped the remaining tears with the sleeve of her tunic, "I do see."

Caleb turned her around, "Look over there."

Nava looked to where he was pointing. About 300 yards away, a young woman stood outside one of the caves, looking up into the sky.

"Who is that?" asked Nava.

"That is Miriam, the mother of the child. They are staying in the cave, recovering from her time of giving birth."

"Oh, my," said Nava. "She looks so young and so petite. She is lovely."

"Yes, she is. I thought the same thing when I first saw her. That night, when the Angels appeared to us, I told Erez that we had to return home to Bethlehem immediately. He did not believe me at first. Fortunately, Nathan convinced him that I was not seeing things, though I still think he does not believe all of it. But I give him credit. He agreed to move our flocks here temporarily.

Nathan and I came right away, traveling here during the night. By the time we arrived, the baby had already been born, but we helped make the cave more suitable for them. A woman named Abigail had come from the village to help Miriam. We built a fire, brought lots of fresh straw and water from our old well and food for them."

"It must be hard to be in such a place," Nava said.

"Yes, it has been used as a stable for years and years. It is warm, though. We are helping them, providing food and water and fresh meat. We don't bother them during the day. This evening, I will take you and Farad to see them."

~ ~ ~ ~

Nava saw to her father Amos' needs the rest of the day. As late afternoon arrived, she got some clean clothing and walked a half-mile into the hill country to a stream with a small wading pool. It was a private place where she could bathe. The feeling of the fresh water and the warm sun restored her. But it was more than that; being back in Bethlehem restored her. She wished Aaron was still there. They would have wed. They would be lovers and would have children of their own. Was it too late for her for the happiness of married life, for the happiness her own family would give her?

She hoped not.

Chapter 21

After supper, Caleb told Nava and Farad to get ready, and they started for the cave. It was a cool evening, especially since dusk was now descending beyond the horizon of the distant hills to the west. As they neared the cave entrance, a warm glow was coming from inside, and smoke was rising from the large natural hole in the top of the cave.

Caleb peered in, "Hello, Miriam, Josef? It is Caleb. I have some special visitors."

"Come in, Caleb," Josef said.

Caleb went in, gesturing for Nava and Farad to follow. Nava was amazed. The cave entrance was not large, but it opened up wide and tall as soon as she stepped inside. It was a spacious area, and she could see how it could have been a stable. It could easily hold several cows and many sheep comfortably, with room to spare. The fire was going strong in the middle, right below the hole in the ceiling. To the left of the fire, further back, Nava could see a woman lying down, sleeping. Next to her was a manger filled with straw. As the Angel had said, a sleeping baby was wrapped in swaddling clothing.

Josef put his finger to his lips, signaling for them to whisper. He waved for them to come to the right side of the cave. There were several logs and a few wooden stools. Josef gestured for them all to sit.

Nava marveled at the youthfulness of Josef. He was very tan, with dark eyes and deep brown hair. He was medium height and strong, with ruddy hands that seemed like they had already worked an entire lifetime.

"Who have you brought to see us, Caleb?"

"This is my granddaughter, the one I told you about. Her name is Nava."

Josef smiled warmly, "Hello, Nava. You are welcome here. And who is with you?"

Nava turned, "This is Farad. He is the steward of Kings from Persia. They are coming here to see you."

Josef's brow furrowed. "Coming here, when?"

"Soon, I think," She turned to Farad.

"Have no fear, Josef," Farad said. "My Lords, the Kings, come to honor the child. We know too that this child is the Messiah, the Savior long-awaited by your people."

Josef's face relaxed as he exhaled loudly. "So much has happened."

Caleb asked him to share his story.

"I met Miriam a year ago in Nazareth. I had known of her. She is several years younger than me. But when she came of age, I noticed her more. We were betrothed. But then she told me she was expecting a baby, and she told me of the Angel who visited her. I wanted to believe her, and yet, how could I? I am human, too." But then, Josef looked up, and a wonder came over his face. He continued, "That night in a dream, an Angel appeared to me and said, 'Josef, do not be afraid to take Miriam as your wife. She has conceived by the power of the Holy Spirit." Josef looked at her, smiling, then turned back to the men. "Then, the census demanded that we come to Bethlehem because my ancestors lived here."

Caleb said, "Josef, the Angel we saw also said to us, 'Do not be afraid.' It just occurred to me that this is the message this child will bring to the world."

"What message is that Grandfather?"

"That we don't have to be afraid anymore. God is with us." He smiled, his old face looking so strong in the firelight. He looked intently into Nava's eyes and repeated, "We don't have to be afraid anymore."

Nava saw Josef nod in agreement; Farad, too, was deep in thought.

"Can I see the child?" Nava asked.

"Yes," Josef replied, "but stay as quiet as you can because they are both resting."

Nava got up and walked over, with Farad treading quietly behind her. She stepped past the fire, then took a few more steps and stopped, looking down at the sleeping baby. Farad walked up next to her and looked down. Nava thought, *How can such a small child change the world?* But then she realized that babies are the only things that always change everything. They are God's way of constantly renewing the world.

She looked at Miriam, peacefully asleep on a bed of straw, cuddled under a blanket. It seemed so wonderful and natural, even in the midst of a cave. Nava felt a deep longing to be a mother herself. She wondered if Farad would stay when the Kings left. She quietly turned, looking into Farad's eyes, then stepped away.

Caleb rose and said quietly, "We will come back tomorrow."

He turned, "Goodbye, Josef."

Josef warmly waved goodbye without saying anything.

Chapter 22

Early the following morning, Nava anxiously headed out of the tents and away from the caves toward the village. There was someone she had to visit. Leah lived with her parents in the middle of the village, not far from where Nava had lived. She had been afraid to go and see her, embarrassed that she was still not married and had wasted so many years. But hearing her grandfather's words last night gave her courage.

When she arrived at the home, Leah's mother answered the door. She exclaimed, "Nava! Oh, my dear girl. It is so good to see you."

Nava hugged her warmly, and they talked for a few minutes. Leah's mother said, "Leah has married and moved."

" Where did she move to?" Nava said, suddenly disappointed she might not see her friend.

"Oh, not far. She lives in a small valley near the outskirts of the village. Her husband bought the house. They have two small children."

Nava's face lit up. "Oh, good. Can you show me?"

"Why sure I can. Come with me."

Leah's mother took her down the village road for about half a mile, then pointed down into a valley. There were several homes near each other. "Leah's home is the one with the wheel leaning against the front of the house."

"Oh, thank you," Nava said as she hugged her and said goodbye.

Nava went down a dirt road that wound its way down a hillside and cut through the homes in the valley. She went to the house with the wheel and knocked. In a moment, Leah opened the door.

"Nava!" she screamed as she burst out the door, hugging her tightly.

"Leah, I missed you!"

Leah exclaimed, barely able to contain her excitement, "Not like I have missed you. How are you?"

Just then, a little girl with long dark brown hair, wearing a dress, ran up and hugged Leah's leg. "Oh, Nava, this is my little Gabriella. She is four years old."

"Oh, she is so beautiful," Nava said as she knelt and smiled at her.

"Who are you?" the girl asked.

"I am your mommy's friend, Nava."

"Hi, Nava."

"Hi to you, Gabriella."

"Come in. I want you to meet my son. He is sleeping."

Leah ushered her into the room that doubled as a dining room and living area. Steps led upstairs to a loft where the family slept. A wooden crib was in the corner of the room by the fireplace. Leah peeked inside, then waved for Nava to come over. Leah whispered, "This is Gershon. He turned one year old a few months ago."

"Oh, he is so beautiful," Nava said. Gershon stirred and stretched, then opened his eyes. "Oh, look who is awake," Leah said as she reached down and picked him up. Gershon rubbed his eyes, looking at Nava.

"Hello, Gershon," Nava said as he turned away, hiding his face.

"He is acting shy, Nava."

Nava looked out the back window. A four-foot-high stone wall surrounded a small courtyard outside the back door. "Oh, what a nice courtyard you have. The children can play there."

"Yes, I am glad it is enclosed."

Nava walked out the back door into the courtyard, followed by Leah and her children. She looked over the back wall. "Oh, look, there is the hill outside of the village. We are camped not far over that hill."

Nava was unsure if she should tell her friend about everything happening, but she decided protecting Miriam and Josef's privacy was more important. She would wait and ask permission first.

Over the next two hours, she and Leah sat in the small walled courtyard, catching up, playing with the children, eating, and drinking tea. Nava marveled at Leah's children. When Aaron had died, something inside died with her. She imagined she would never marry and never have children. Ever since then, she had lost interest in children and rarely interacted with them in any meaningful way. But Gabrielle and Gershon were so beautiful, innocent, and special. It made her wish she had not spent so many years grieving. The desire to have her own children flickered within her, a hope she had once held but had forgotten.

Finally, she said, "I must go now, but I will return tomorrow."

"Oh, we are leaving tomorrow," Leah said.

"Where are you going?"

"Not far. Because of the Roman census, we have to travel to Beersheba. It is only a few days' journey there, and then we will return."

"Oh, I am sorry. I will see you when you get back then." Nava decided the news could wait.

They hugged and laughed and said goodbye, smiling at each other and thrilled to be reunited after so long.

As Nava left, a wave of emotion swept over her. She had stayed away too long, and she vowed in her heart to come back here more often, if not for good.

Chapter 23

Nava returned to the hillside encampment set up by her Uncle Erez. Farad was out in the fields helping with the flocks. He had decided it would be a better use of his time than sitting around. There was still no word from the Kings. Amos was doing better, though still bedridden. Nava went in to talk with him. "Father, I got to see Leah and her children."

"That's wonderful. How is she?"

"She is well. She has two children."

"I am happy to hear that."

Uncle Erez came in, interrupting him. "Amos, I am having my men take you to my house in Hebron for a while. The women can care for you there. I am worried you are going to grow worse here. Your healing is progressing too slowly."

Amos nodded, "Perhaps it will be best."

Erez added, "Nava, you will go with him."

She stood up immediately, "No, I am not going anywhere."

Erez's face grew cross, "You don't have a choice, Nava. I am in charge of this family and this camp. You are going."

She turned to her father, "Father, tell him no. I am staying here. I am waiting for Leah to return also."

Amos said, "Let me talk to Uncle Erez alone."

Nava stormed out. Not far away, her grandfather was sitting, smoking a pipe. Nava ran up to him. "Grandfather, please. Uncle Erez is trying to send me to Hebron."

Caleb's face furrowed, "What? Why?"

"I don't know. Because I am a woman. Please, talk to him."

"Where is he?"

"In my father's tent."

Caleb set his pipe down and went in. Nava got a little closer and listened. A long and heated discussion seemed to end with Uncle Erez storming out. Caleb came out too, with a cross look on his face, but then his eyes met Nava's, and he smiled. "You can stay, Nava, but they are taking your father back to our home so he can heal more quickly."

Nava hugged him tightly, "Thank you, Grandfather."

~ ~ ~ ~

That evening, Nava said goodbye to her father and then went to find Farad. They walked outside the large camp and sat under a tree on top of the hillside, watching the sun begin to set. It was now the tenth day since they got word to come to Bethlehem and their third day since arriving.

She saw Farad near the outskirts of the camp and waved for him to come and join her. He sat down next to her, admiring the sun with her. She asked, "Do you think the Kings will come soon?"

"Yes, I imagine tomorrow. What of you, Nava? Are you going to stay here longer?"

"Yes, I will stay as long as my grandfather does."

It was quiet for a while, and Nava asked, "Do you have anyone back home, Farad?"

"You mean, like a woman waiting for me?"

"Yes," she said shyly.

"There is someone, but I am unsure about her."

"Oh, and why is that?"

"Because she has a nose as long as a carrot."

Nava burst out laughing, and within a moment, Farad laughed, too. "No, Nava, there is no one waiting for me."

Neither of them spoke for a few minutes. Then, Nava leaned over and kissed him when the silence grew loud. He kissed her back, and they kissed for several long moments, then drew apart. Nava blushed and smiled, looking out at the setting sun. She had not kissed anyone since Aaron. Kissing Farad made her stomach do flips. She felt light and carefree and full of a nervous but pleasant energy.

"Nava?" came a voice from a distance. It was her grandfather. Nava smiled and jumped up, "I have to go."

"Go ahead. I will talk to you tomorrow."

"Are you going into the fields again?" she asked.

"Yes, your uncle said I have to earn my keep."

Nava rolled her eyes, then ran down the hill, shouting, "Coming, Grandfather."

Chapter 24

At Herod's Palace, Kings Balthazar, Melchior, and Caspar sat on luxurious couches, being brought exquisite dishes by King Herod's myriad of servants. Before them, seated up a level, lay King Herod. King Herod was a large man. Fat, anyone would say, but never to his face. Years of laying on his couches and eating enough food for two or three men had sickened his body and clouded his mind. His wide beard covered his wide face, and when he laughed, his entire neck and stomach would jiggle like jelly. Normally, though, he was angry and cross in dealing with his soldiers and palace servants.

Herod was already aware from his vast network of informants of the questions the Kings had been asking in their long approach to Jerusalem. They had asked travelers along the road about a newborn King of the Jews.

Herod meant to test them.

He sipped his goblet of wine and smiled, asking, "So, my fellow Kings, tell me why have you come to Jerusalem?"

Balthazar replied, "We followed a star, King Herod. We spotted the star over a year ago while we were in Persia. This star seemed to be a sign of an immense labor in the Heavens. There is a text in the ancient Jewish writings that says, 'I shall see him, but not now; I shall behold him, but not soon; there shall come a Star out of Jacob, and a scepter shall rise out of Israel.'" Balthazar turned to his friend and continued, "Over a year ago, my friend, Melchior, came to me and told me he had discovered this star too. So, we set out to find it."

"Have you found it?" Herod asked, with a wide smile on his face.

"Why yes. You have not noticed it?"

"No," Herod said in a disturbed tone. He rarely did anything at night except lie in bed with one of his concubines from his harem.

Melchior said, "It is high in the sky south of Jerusalem."

"South, you say," Herod said, "And you saw it over a year ago. Is that what you said?"

"Yes, it was last year, after the Harvest Season, over 15 moons ago."

"I see," Herod said, mentally noting how old this baby might already be. There would be no ruler in Israel other than him.

Just then, Herod's steward bowed low, "King Herod, the men you summoned have arrived."

"Take them into the hall," Herod said. He said to the Kings, "You will excuse me. This will only take a moment. It is, I am afraid, official business I must attend to."

Moments later, Herod walked into the Great Hall of his palace wearing a flowing maroon and gold-laced robe that hid his girth. There were three men, all members of the Sanhedrin, the leaders of the Jewish community. They all wore black robes with white and black colored head coverings. One of them carried a cane to help him walk.

Herod glared at them for a moment, ensuring they were aware of his seriousness, but then he smiled as was his way of disarming them. "Good evening, Levi and Zerah, and oh, I am sorry, I have forgotten your name."

"Gilead, King Herod."

"Oh, yes, Gilead."

Herod went right to business. "I need to know what the prophecy is. I have heard in the past about the Messiah."

Levi answered right away, "In the book of Micah, it says, 'But you, Bethlehem Ephrathah, though you are little among the thousands of Judah, yet out of you shall come forth to Me, the One to be Ruler in Israel, whose goings forth are from of old, from everlasting.'"

"Ruler?" Herod said, scoffing, "In Israel? But I am the ruler in Israel." Herod watched their reactions carefully.

Levi looked at his associates with a look of concern. He said, "I am sure, good King Herod, this refers to some future time. You need not worry."

Herod's eyes narrowed, "I will worry about what I want to worry about!"

There was silence as Herod watched all their eyes lower to the floor, seemingly at once. Herod asked, "How certain are you that this... prophecy would be accurate?"

"I don't understand, King Herod."

"Bethlehem!" he shouted. "Is it accurate?"

Levi nodded, "Yes, King Herod. It would be accurate."

Herod turned, "Thank you for coming. That is all I need." He turned and returned to rejoin the other Kings.

When Herod sat back down, he smiled warmly and said, "So, do you know where this newborn future King of Israel will be born?"

Balthazar replied, "We do not, King Herod."

Herod looked up, putting his finger to his lips as if summoning some memory. He said, "I remember an old text that refers to Bethlehem as the place. That is... south of here. Perhaps it is there?"

"Which text are you referring to?" Balthazar asked.

"Oh, the book of... what is it again? Oh yes, Micah. I will have it brought to you tonight in your chambers."

Balthazar looked at the other Kings and nodded, "Then that is where we must go."

"Yes," Herod said. "Go to Bethlehem and find this child and come back to me so that I too may go and honor him."

The three Kings all rose as Herod stayed on his couch. They all nodded, "Thank you for the banquet, good King Herod. We will leave early in the morning."

Herod watched them leave his presence, and a deep, angry frown came over his face. He summoned the Centurion.

Sometime later, when the Centurion arrived, Herod said, "Follow them and report back to me their movements. Do not let yourselves be seen."

Chapter 25

Early in the morning, Nava was awakened by the sound of the noisy flocks of nearby sheep. She went outside just in time to see her grandfather, Farad, and the other men taking the sheep further away from the village in search of fresh pasture. She went about the duties that Uncle Erez had assigned to her around camp, spreading fresh hay in the donkey pen, feeding the chickens he had bought from a local farmer, and bringing water from the nearby well to each of the four tents. After she finished, she made herself breakfast of fruit and cheese.

She heard a commotion coming from the distant village and set off on foot to see what was happening. It took a while to go down the hillside and through the valley, eventually getting to where the road from the countryside turned to the wider main road of the village.

When she rounded the turn into the village, she saw what was making all the commotion. It was the three Kings and their entourage of camels, oxen, and carts. Balthazar, Melchior, and Caspar were all seated high upon their camels in front of the long line. The entire caravan had stopped, and some of the men were talking. A growing crowd came out of their houses to see the unusual spectacle.

Nava smiled and kept walking toward them, not wanting to cause any scene, as she was still unsure if it was okay to reveal to anyone what was happening.

When she was close to the Kings, she waved. Balthazar saw her and waved, crying out, "Nava!"

Nava bowed, then rose with a smile on her face. She put her finger to her lips, then motioned for him, and them all, to follow. She turned and started walking back down the road where she had come from. She tried to stay to the side of the road, not wishing to act like she was leading a parade of camels, oxen, and Kings, but she was. She laughed at the thought, and as she passed the turn-off road that led down into the valley where Leah lived, she wished Leah was here today to see the kindly Kings.

Once the caravan got outside the village and turned into the countryside, the townspeople began returning to their homes, realizing the Kings must just be passing through. Nava kept going down through the valley and up the next hillside, and then she waited until the Kings caught up to her.

"Good morning, King Balthazar, King Melchior, and King Caspar," she said with a wide smile.

Melchior said, "Good morning to you, Nava. Where is Farad?"

Nava laughed, saying, "My uncle has put him to work taking care of the flocks."

Melchior smiled, "Have you found the newborn child?"

Nava tightened her lips, and her eyes could not help but shine as she nodded and said, "Come, I will show you."

The three Kings looked at each other, then kept going, waving for their caravan to follow. Soon, they were up on top of the hill and onto the plateau where the caves were. Nava marveled as the scene unfolded. Bethlehem had never had Kings such as these, dressed in flowing royal robes, riding on top of tall camels. The collection of soldiers, servants, and oxen with them only magnified the immensity of the scene.

Nava ran down the road a way and pointed to a distant field. "Put out your camels, other beasts, and men over there in that field. This way, you will not be too close to their cave. We are trying to give the little family as much privacy as possible."

Balthazar asked, "That is a good idea. Where are they?"

Nava pointed to a distant group of caves. "They are way over there, in one of those caves, well, actually, one is a stable. It is very comfortable for them."

Balthazar looked on, his eyes showing the confusion he felt. He looked to the other Kings, who also showed the same concern. Finally, Nava said, "I will go ahead and see if they can see you now."

As Nava had instructed, Balthazar waved for his caravan to continue to the field.

Nava then turned and ran to the cave. She had never been there alone and was unsure she should disturb them. So she went to the vast entrance and said, "Hello?"

Josef came out. "Hi, you are Caleb's granddaughter, but I have forgotten your name."

"Nava," she said. Then, she pointed into the distance, "The Kings my grandfather and I told you about are here. They said they have gifts for you, your wife, and the child."

Josef looked at them cautiously, thinking. "Come in, Nava. I want to ask Miriam."

Nava followed him in. Miriam sat comfortably on a pile of fresh straw covered by a large blanket. She was nursing the baby. Nava knelt in front of her and smiled, "Good morning. My name is Nava."

"Good morning, Nava. I am Miriam."

"Oh, it is so nice to meet you," thinking how beautiful and young she was to have had a child.

Miriam smiled at her and glanced down at the infant suckling at her breast. Josef said, "Miriam, the kings Caleb told me about are here. They would like to see us."

"Oh, I see. Are they here now?"

"They are putting their camels in a distant field. I asked them to," Nava said.

Miriam said, "Nava, go and tell them we will be ready in an hour. I want to finish caring for this little one and get ready myself."

Nava beamed, "Okay, I will tell them."

Miriam said, "You come with them too, Nava. I want you to be here. And bring your friend that Josef told me about, Farad?"

"I will. He works for the kings."

"So, I have heard," Miriam said, "Thank you for your help."

Nava nodded and scampered up and went to tell the kings.

Chapter 26

The Centurion marched into the main hall where Herod was seated on his Throne. He stood at attention. "Great King. They are camped outside of Bethlehem."

"So, it is true," Herod said, his face bearing a half-scowl. "Have you identified who the child is?"

"No, not as of yet. We have not been able to get close enough."

"How many people live in Bethlehem?"

"There are approximately 3,000 King Herod, but many more are there now because of the Census. So the village has more people than normal, as many as double."

Herod stiffened momentarily, "Double, that may make things more difficult."

"What do you mean?" the Centurion asked.

"Never mind what I mean." Herod glared, "Go and see if you can find out who this child is and exactly where he is!"

~ ~ ~ ~

Farad and Nava walked along solemnly from the field where the kings had camped toward the cave. Behind them were Balthazar, Melchior, and Caspar. Each of the kings carried something in their hands. Nava came to the entrance and called, "Josef, Miriam, it is Nava. We are here."

"Come in, Nava."

Nava walked in with Farad and stepped aside to allow the kings to advance. Miriam was standing next to Josef, holding the infant in her arms. She wore a light brown tunic tied at the waist with a strip of dark brown cloth and brown sandals. Her head was covered with a blue head covering. Josef wore a plain, darker brown tunic with a brown leather belt.

Nava watched the kings bow low before Miriam, Josef, and the child. Then, one by one, they told Miriam and Josef their names. Then, they gave Josef gifts. Nava's eyes widened as Gold, Frankincense, and Myrrh were handed to Josef. She understood that each gift held immense value and realized that the little family probably needed the money. Now, with what they had been given, they would have enough for several years if needed.

Balthazar asked, "May we hold the child?"

Miriam nodded.

She handed the swaddled young baby to Balthazar. "What is his name?"

"Yeshua," Miriam said.

"Look at him," Balthazar said proudly, showing him to his fellow kings. Melchior took the child into his arms. He closed his eyes, and Nava saw a tear fall down his cheek. He then handed the child to Caspar, who held him, smiling, then kissed him softly on the forehead before handing the baby back to his Miriam.

Balthazar looked around, "How can the King of Kings, the Messiah, be born here in this cave, in this stable? Look at his bed. It is nothing more than a feeding trough for animals."

Melchior wiped another tear from his eye, "Yes, he is born in humility to show us the way to live."

Caspar said in a voice that held an unmistakable prophetic tone, "He will be a King, not only of Kings but for all people, rich and poor alike, with no distinction. Every person will matter to him."

Nava was amazed.

She looked at Farad and smiled, and for a moment, she worried. The kings would be leaving before long. Would Farad be going with them? Would he, perhaps, want her to go to?

Chapter 27

The next day, Farad came to wake Nava. He whispered, "Nava, wake up. I want to talk to you."

She lifted her head from her pillow and saw her grandfather was still asleep on the other side of the tent. Her heart leaped within her. This was the moment she had been hoping for. Farad was going to tell her something important, perhaps something that would align their futures as one. She quietly got up and went outside to talk with him.

Farad motioned for her to follow, and they walked a little distance from the tent. He turned, and she could see that he did not bear good news by the look on his face. "What is it, Farad?"

"There is news. King Herod has some spies here watching us."

"How do you know?" Nava asked.

"I saw them last night."

"Why would he send spies?"

"Balthazar fears that Herod will want to harm the child. So, none of us will visit the cave today. Tell your grandfather."

"Did they see you?" Nava asked.

"I don't think so. I saw them approach after we had left the cave. I believe they only saw that we were camped outside the village."

"What are you going to do?"

Farad gestured to the south, "They are down in the valley now, a half-mile from here, sleeping behind a grove of trees. We are leaving tonight after dark and going back to Persia by route through the desert. King Caspar had a dream warning us not to return to Herod. So, when it is time to leave, we will take them as prisoners and bring them with us for a while. We will not harm them. We will release them when we are far away from here."

"Leaving, but… can I go with you?"

Farad lowered his glance, "Nava, you are a beautiful woman and must stay here in your country. You would be considered a foreigner in Persia. Life would be difficult."

She stepped closer, "But, I thought we liked each other?"

"I do like you very much, Nava. I will always cherish our days together and our kiss, but I must go." Farad hugged her, then went back to his camp.

Nava wandered to her tent. She had thought that love might exist or even grow between her and Farad, but now, she understood she had been foolish to think it. She went inside her tent, crawled under the blankets, and began to weep softly.

~ ~ ~ ~

It was late morning when her grandfather came into the tent again. "Nava, aren't you feeling well today? Uncle Erez said he wants you to take care of your duties."

Nava slowly opened her eyes, keeping her head under the blanket. The old darkness of depression had returned with a vengeance today. It had disappeared over the last few weeks, but it hurt to even think again. "Grandfather, I don't feel good," she said under the blanket.

"What is wrong, Nava?" he asked, kneeling beside her. He gently pulled back the blanket and saw her reddened eyes and a deep frown. "What happened, Nava?"

"The kings and Farad, they are leaving tonight."

"I see," he said, "Why?"

"Something about King Herod. He has spies here."

Caleb's brow furrowed. He said, "Wait here, Nava. I will go and speak to them. I want to find out what is happening."

A while later, her grandfather returned. Nava sat up, feeling embarrassed that she was still sleeping. "What happened, Grandfather?"

"I spoke with the kings. We all agree that Miriam, Josef, and the child should leave late tonight, long after the kings are gone. Uncle Erez said they will take the cart you came in, and Farad will let them use the oxen to pull it."

"Why do they have to leave?"

"They feel it will be safer. I am sending one of my carrier pigeons to my brother in Jerusalem. He has a family member who works in Herod's palace. If there is any trouble, he can send me a message right away."

"Oh, Grandfather. Will there be trouble?"

"I don't know, Nava. King Herod is an evil and vengeful man. I am afraid there could be."

Nava's worry deepened. Her grandfather said, "Nava, get up and get ready. You and I have to go speak to Miriam and Josef."

Chapter 28

A short while later, Nava and her grandfather went to the cave. Caleb called, "Josef, Miriam, may we speak with you?"

Miriam came to the cave entrance, holding her finger to her lips. "Caleb, Nava, hi. Josef is asleep. He was up all night with the baby."

"Is the baby okay?" Nava asked.

"Oh, yes, he was just fussy last night."

"May we come in, Miriam? It is important."

"Yes," she said without hesitation.

As she turned, she said, "Josef is stirring. Here, both of you sit." Miriam pointed to two wooden stools near the front of the cave. "I will go wake him. I am sure he will need a few minutes to wake up."

Nava and Caleb sat down, waiting. Finally, Miriam returned, holding the baby. "Nava, will you hold little Yeshua while I do a few things?"

"Oh, yes, I would like that."

Miriam laid the child into Nava's arms. Nava looked up into Miriam's eyes and saw something beautiful, strong and yet vulnerable simultaneously. Miriam paused momentarily and watched little Yeshua turn his head, looking up at Nava. "I think he likes you, Nava."

Nava wiped a tear from her eye. She did not know why, but she felt overwhelmed holding him.

Miriam turned and went back to the back of the cave. Nava could see that Josef was getting up, too.

Caleb said, "Nava, what a great privilege we have been given."

"I know, Grandfather, but I don't know what I will do. I failed to help my father, causing him injury. I thought Farad liked me, even loved me, and he is leaving without me. I just feel lost." A few tears escaped from her eyes. She continued, trembling, "Long ago, a voice within me told me to go to the well to help Aaron, and I did not listen. If I was there, he would not have died."

She began to cry softly

Caleb put his arm around her and said, "My dear Nava, remember the words of King Solomon.

There is an appointed time for everything
and a time for every affair under the heavens.
A time to give birth and a time to die;
a time to plant and a time to uproot the plant.
A time to kill and a time to heal;
a time to tear down and a time to build.
A time to weep and a time to laugh;
a time to mourn and a time to dance.
A time to scatter stones and a time to gather them;
a time to embrace and a time to be far from embraces.
A time to seek and a time to lose;
a time to keep and a time to cast away.
A time to rend and a time to sew;
a time to be silent and a time to speak.
A time to love and a time to hate;
a time of war and a time of peace.

When he finished, he said, "Nava, you need not be afraid. You stood up to Uncle Erez and stayed here with us. Keep following the voice inside of you."

"But I feel so lost," she lamented.

"Now, Nava, listen to me. I have prayed for you, and my heart tells me that a day will come when the God of Israel will call you out of darkness and into a new day of light and hope. I promise you this."

" Thank you," she said, wiping a tear and leaning against his shoulder, carefully holding the baby tight.

"Look," her grandfather said, motioning to the child in her arms. The baby was looking up at her, his eyes more open than she had ever seen. "I think he heard us. He looks like he understands."

Nava marveled and kissed the child on the forehead.

Just then, Miriam and Josef came over, and Nava handed the baby back to Miriam.

"What is going on, Caleb?" Josef asked.

Caleb stood and said, "We fear there will be trouble from King Herod. The Kings are leaving tonight under cover of darkness. They say you should head toward Egypt. They said that Herod would not look for you there. Erez wants you both to leave, too. He will give you our cart, and the kings will give you their oxen. Erez and two of his men will go with you for several nights to ensure you get far away safely. The rest of us will take the flocks along the roadway further south of here as a diversion and to slow anyone who wants to follow."

Miriam touched her heart and closed her eyes, sighing visibly. Josef pulled her close, "Don't worry, Miriam. God will protect us."

~ ~ ~ ~

In the late afternoon, Nava suddenly thought of Leah. She needed to warn her. She went up to the high hillside where Farad had kissed her. From there, she could barely see the back of Leah's house. There did not seem to be any activity. She calculated the date when Leah had left for Beersheba to be counted in the census and determined she would not be back for perhaps a few more days. But she needed to be sure, so she walked down to the village and went to the house. She knocked on the door and peered in the windows. They were still gone.

Chapter 29

The day was long, and darkness came early again. Nava stayed outside her tent, watching Farad and his men mill about. She saw them bringing two men bound with ropes and put them into a tent. Herod's spies had been caught, as Farad foretold. Farad and the men resumed packing their tents.

As Nava watched from a distance, she was glad she was not going with them. Her grandfather's words had given her hope. There would be a future for her. There would be a time for her, a time of love and new life. She trusted this. But it was more than her grandfather's words. Looking into the eyes of Miriam and holding the baby, Yeshua had somehow changed her.

She felt strong again.

Soon, the caravan of kings and their men and beasts could be faintly heard in the darkness, slowly moving toward the southeast, away from the outskirts of Bethlehem.

A half-hour later, Uncle Erez's men finished packing up their camp. He and two of his men led the oxen and cart over to the cave.

Miriam and Josef came out, holding the infant Yeshua, and entered the cart.

Nava ran to her tent and retrieved the sword Aaron had given her long ago. She showed it to Josef and said, "I will place this in the cart if you need it."

"Thank you for everything, Nava."

Nava went over to the other side. She took Miriam's hand and said, "Goodbye, Miriam."

Miriam handed the baby to Josef and stepped down. She hugged Nava tightly and smiled into her eyes, saying, "You are a brave woman, Nava. I am praying for you."

Nava felt her eyes water. She did not want to say goodbye. She wanted to go with them, to continue this grand adventure she had been on, but she had to step away.

The cart started down the road. Nava walked away and stood by her grandfather, watching them fade into the distance. It reminded her of just twelve days earlier when they had left Sidon, and she had watched her mother fade into the distance.

Chapter 30

As they were watching them leave, the carrier pigeon her grandfather had sent to Jerusalem earlier flew down and landed in front of them.

Caleb quickly picked it up and untied the message from its leg. He unfurled it and began to read. Nava watched his eyes race down the tiny scroll as his expression grew worried. Finally, he looked up with a look of shock.

"What is it, Grandfather?"

"Herod's soldiers are coming," he exclaimed, "They are coming to kill all the young males in Bethlehem."

Nava's face froze.

Caleb yelled, "Erez, wait." He ran ahead.

Nava turned to look at the village. She ran as fast as she could up to the hillside. She needed to see Leah's house once more. When she reached the top, her heart dropped.

A lamp was lit in the home.

Leah and her family had returned.

Nava ran back to the road and ran after her grandfather and uncle, who were talking hastily as they kept the cart with Josef and Miriam moving.

"Grandfather," she shouted, "We have to warn Leah."

Her grandfather turned and looked at her, but his eyes conveyed urgency. He quickly turned back toward Erez, pointing off the side of the road, and shouted, "Go off the road and head into the desert, Erez. Quickly!"

Nava tugged at her grandfather's arm, shouting, "Grandfather, please, we have to warn Leah!"

Erez replied impatiently, "There is no time, Nava. We have to help Miriam and Josef. We are wasting time!"

"There *is* time!" she pleaded, turning her eyes back toward the city.

"We cannot!" Erez shouted, putting an end to the matter with his stern tone. He gritted his teeth and pointed toward the village, "Look, the soldiers are already coming."

Nava turned. In the distance, she saw what looked like up to a hundred torches moving slowly along the road at the other end of the horizon, closing in on the village of Bethlehem. She turned back to Miriam and saw the growing worry in her eyes. Their eyes locked, and Nava saw more. There was calm courage in Miriam's eyes, a calm trust, unwilling to yield to the terror they all felt.

Erez shouted, "Caleb, Nava, you will come with us. My men and the flocks will stay on the road."

Nava turned to her grandfather, searching for the courage she needed. His face looked helpless, as she knew he wanted to help her, but somehow, he knew he could not. She thought back to the time so long ago when she had failed to act, when she had failed to go see Aaron, when she had failed to help her father when the bandits attacked them, those times when she had failed to listen to her heart.

Suddenly, she lurched forward and reached into the back of Miriam and Josef's cart. She grabbed Aaron's sword she had laid in there for them.

She needed it now.

"What are you doing?" her grandfather Caleb shouted.

She did not wait. She turned and started running along the dark road back toward Bethlehem.

"Nava," cried Caleb.

He turned to Erez, "Go, now! Hurry! I will go after her."

Erez screamed, "No, Caleb! Stay here!"

Caleb stopped.

Erez shouted down the road, "Nava!"

Erez then started to run after her, then stopped, torn by his duty. In his moment of hesitancy, he watched her disappear into the night. He then ran back to Miriam, Josef, and Caleb. He took the cart off the road into the desert and ordered his other men to clog the road with the flocks.

Caleb walked off the road, pretending to go along, and waited for his moment. He drifted back slightly so his son Erez would not notice, then turned and took off after Nava.

Chapter 31

Nava ran away from the road, down into the long valley that stretched between the caves and the outer edge of the village. It was dark, and the terrain was rough. When she reached the bottom of the hillside, she could see the back courtyard of Leah's house in the distance. A lamp illuminated the back doorway and part of the courtyard. She kept running.

The screaming in the village had already started. Nava peered over the courtyard wall of her lifelong friend Leah's home. Leah's husband was lying on the ground just inside the home, next to the back door. His midsection was blood-stained. He was dying. Nava held her hand to her mouth, terrified.

The next moment, she saw Leah crouched in the opposite corner of the courtyard in front of her children, fending off a Roman soldier. Her arms were spread wide, frantically moving, trying to protect little Gabrielle and Gershon as they hid behind her, screaming in fright.

"No! No! Please, no!" Leah screamed, her face pleading in anguish, her body maneuvering in any way to shield them.

The soldier had his back to Nava, so she quickly placed the sword on top of the wall and then struggled to climb up and over.

She was halfway up when she saw the soldier turn his sword and strike Leah in the head with the handle of it. Leah fell backward, barely conscious. The soldier then reached for the crying little boy, but Leah rose. "No!! She cried as she attacked him, biting his arm. The soldier knocked her off and lifted his sword high, readying it. Finally, Nava crested the wall and jumped down, landing softly, carrying Aaron's sword in hand. She lifted it high and ran straight at the unsuspecting soldier.

The soldier plunged his sword into Leah's chest. In the next moment, Nava plunged her sword, the one Aaron had given her, straight down between the shoulders of the bent-over soldier.

Leah cried out in agony, and so did the soldier.

Nava stepped back and watched them both fall to the side, leaving the terrified, crying children exposed, staring at her. Then, she heard shouting near the front of the house.

More soldiers were coming.

She grabbed Gabrielle and Gershon and picked them up. She ran to the back wall and threw them over it one by one, screaming, "Run! Run into the hills!"

She peered over the wall and saw her grandfather, Caleb. He had just arrived at the bottom of the hill in the back of the house. He stopped, trying to see through the darkness.

Nava shouted, "Take them, Grandfather. Hurry, take them away."

The children stopped, confused, afraid to run into the night, but Nava screamed, "Gabrielle! Gershon! Go with him. Now!"

"What about you!" Caleb yelled frantically, "Come with us!"

"I will! Just go! Hurry!"

Caleb scooped the little boy Gershon into his strong arm, took Gabrielle by the hand, and ran into the night.

Nava sighed with relief. They were safe.

She turned once more to look at Leah. She was dead. Nava felt her heart drop. She had been too late to save her, but she glanced over the wall into the night. She had saved Leah's children. Leah would have wanted that. "Goodbye, my dear friend."

She heard a commotion in the front and tried pulling herself up and over but stumbled back. She turned, looking for something to stand on, and then she saw them.

Two Roman soldiers with swords drawn ran into the courtyard. They looked at their companion with Nava's sword in his back, then up at her, and ran at her. Nava tried to turn and leap onto the wall again but was too late. She felt the terrifying, piercing pain of the cold steel blade plunged into her back, going out of her stomach. She screamed, then fell down in agony.

She wanted to live and restart her life, but it was too late. Her mind began to spin, and the darkness began to waver. It was all over. She was dying.

She felt sad for what might have been.

Her depression that so long haunted her days was gone, but there would be no new day or season of life. She looked over at Leah's lifeless body. She was glad she had saved her children and only hoped they would get away.

She glanced up at the wall and saw her grandfather's face peer over and look down at her.

He had come back.

She tried to lift her hand toward him, but it fell flat into the dust with a thud. She tried to cry out to him, but only a muffled, blood-soaked sound came out.

She closed her eyes.

Chapter 32

Jerusalem
Thirty-Three Years Later

A rugged man wearing a white tunic with a tan prayer shawl over his shoulder stepped from the dark confines into the morning sunlight, taking in a deep awakening breath. His feet were bare, but it mattered not to him. Nothing mattered to him on this morning. He glanced over at the soldiers sleeping nearby, shook his head, and smiled. They would be very surprised in a short while, and he hoped they would not get into too much trouble.

There was much for him to do here, in Jerusalem, this morning. But first, there was somewhere else he had to go. Something he knew that would please his mother.

He closed his eyes, and in the next moment, he was in Bethlehem.

He smiled, looking at the houses and streets he had not seen in ages. Indeed, most people were sleeping, with only a few already up and about their morning rituals. He walked along in the early morning light, periodically waving to the person or two who were also up early this Sunday morning.

He reached the edge of the village and glanced up the hillside to the not-too-distant caves. They were still there, standing strong. He walked up the hillside road and went over to the one he knew was the place where it had all begun. He had been there several times during the past 33 years, always fond of the memories it held for him. He returned and continued down the road, past the caves, to the place further away from the village where the tombs were located.

It all felt desolate as he approached the tombs, and he thought of death. Death itself was desolate, and until now, it was the end. Now, because of what had happened earlier, everything would change.

He paused and looked back toward the village. It was still dawn, and the sun was just beginning to crest over the horizon, shining its warm light on Bethlehem.

He continued onto the pathway that wound through the tombs, not saying a word, thinking about that night so very long ago. His memories of it had been given to him by his mother. She had told him the story countless times when he was a boy. Today, though, he understood the story differently, as if he were there.

When he reached the place, he stood quietly, thinking. This deed he was about to do could wait until he was ready to bring the others, but why should he wait?

She had not waited.

When the danger was near, she had run toward it, not away from it. His mind raced back to the night long ago when he heard Nava cry, "No, I must help them."

He said to himself, "And now, it is my turn to help her."

He stood in front of a tomb, looking at the boulder. He stepped forward and placed his hands along its thick, hewn edges, feeling along the seal. He then stepped back three steps, staring at it for a moment.

Finally, he raised his hand high as if summoning all of the universe into his grasp and shouted, "Nava! Come Forth!"

Everything grew silent. The birds, the wind, the clouds all stood perfectly still, and then it happened.

The heavy stone boulder that had been set there over 30 years earlier quivered, then simply rolled aside and fell into the dust with a loud thud. He looked into the darkness of the hollowed-out cave that was Nava's tomb.

Suddenly, a body walked into the light, covered from head to foot in a dusty burial cloth.

He stepped forward, gently grasped her by the shoulders, and unwrapped the head covering.

Nava's beautiful eyes glistened in the sun. She exclaimed, "What is happening? Who are you?"

"Nava, I am Yeshua. So long ago, I heard your cry, and I have come to give you your reward."

"Yeshua...?" she asked, not sure who he was.

"Yes, remember me, Nava, the infant so long ago in the cave in Bethlehem. Remember my mother, Miriam, and my father, Josef. Remember when you ran to save Leah's children from Herod's soldiers."

It all came rushing back to her as her mouth dropped open, remembering the night, Leah dying on the floor, and the feeling of the sword piercing her back and stomach. Her hands grasped her midsection, and she looked down. There was no sign of anything.

Yeshua waved his hand, and she was suddenly dressed in her clothing. A long brown skirt and a fluffed blouse with a brown vest over it. Her head was adorned with a white covering tied behind her neck, which hung down like a beautiful veil. Yeshua held his hand out, "I am taking you to Heaven, Nava, but first, I have something to show you."

Nava looked into his eyes. They were eyes that could be trusted, eyes that held peace, eyes that seemed to hold the secrets of life, the secrets of the ages.

She reached out and took his hand.

Chapter 33

In the next moment, they were in front of a house in the middle of Bethlehem, yet somehow, they could not be seen. Men, women, and children were beginning to wake and leave their homes, busy with the morning hustle of life in the village. Then, a man came out of a house with three children trailing behind. The man went directly across the street and knocked on the door of what appeared to be his neighbor.

Nava suddenly recognized the house.

It was Leah's house.

A woman answered, nearly the same age as the man. "Come in, come in," the woman said.

The young man and his children happily walked in.

Yeshua motioned for Nava to follow, and they followed them unnoticed. The man sat down at a table set with plates and cups. Four other children were there, giddily laughing with the children who had just come in. Another man was already sitting at the head of the table, which Nava realized was the woman's husband. The woman was busy putting fruit, cheese, and freshly baked bread on the table, now holding seven children.

"Who are these people?" Nava asked Yeshua with a voice growing in hope.

Yeshua said to her, "Nava, that woman is Leah's daughter, Gabrielle, and that man who came from across the street with his children, that is Gershon, Leah's son. Your bravery saved them on that night so long ago. Gabrielle has four children, and Gershon has three."

"Oh, how beautiful," Nava said. "What happened to Leah?"

Yeshua lowered his head, "Leah did not survive that night, though before she died, she saw that you saved her children. Don't worry about her, though. She believes in me, and they who believe in me will never die. You will see her again, in Heaven, as in the days to come, many shall be raised to new life, to everlasting life."

Nava began to weep softly. She scanned the table, filled with two families her heroic actions had helped to save. Finally, she looked up into Yeshua's eyes and said, "My Grandfather Caleb was right. You truly are the Christ, the Messiah, just like the kings and shepherds said."

Yeshua's smiled widely, "Yes, I am. Take my hand. We are going to Heaven now and to a special house where someone you know lives."

Nava took his hand, and within a moment, she felt a whirlwind of air as if they were in the clouds, and they descended onto a grassy hillside that looked down upon a beautiful sparkling lake. They were in front of a home with white plastered walls and a neat, newly thatched roof.

Yeshua walked to the front door and knocked.

In a moment, the door opened, and a man looked out, smiling. "Yeshua?"

Yeshua stepped aside, and Nava stepped into the doorway.

"Nava!" he said, his voice trembling with happiness.

"Grandfather!" she exclaimed.

"Oh, my dear granddaughter. I have missed you all these years." He turned to Yeshua, exclaiming, "Thank you, Lord."

Yeshua said, "I have one more surprise for you, Nava."

Yeshua said to Caleb, "My dear friend, Caleb. Do you remember long ago in the cave in Bethlehem, you told Nava that one day God would call her out of the darkness into a marvelous new light?"

"Yes, I remember," Caleb said.

Yeshua raised his hand and said, "I heard your voice that night, Caleb. Behold."

He pointed, and Caleb and Nava turned.

A young man was sitting in the grass by the edge of the water. He looked at his hands, turning them over as if he had not seen them in a long time. Then, finally, he stood up and looked down. He wore a simple dark brown tunic with a leather belt around his waist and sandals on his feet.

Nava knew him in an instant. She took off running down the hillside.

"Who is it?" Caleb asked.

Yeshua smiled. "You will see."

As Nava drew nearer, she began shouting, "Aaron! Aaron!"

The young man turned, and his eyes widened as if he suddenly realized who was calling him. He, too, started running up the hillside. "Nava!" he cried.

They ran into each other's arms, twirling around, falling, laughing, and hugging. "Aaron, I have found you. Oh, Aaron, I love you."

He held her still, peering into her eyes, then kissed her warmly. "I love you, Nava. We are alive again."

Nava exclaimed, "We are, Aaron, and this time it is forever." She grabbed him tightly, "Oh, I will never let you go."

They clung tightly to each other, kissing incessantly, the tears on their faces mingling.

Up at the house, Caleb wiped a tear from his eye, turned to Yeshua, and noticed he was wiping a tear from his cheek, too.

They both smiled and looked away again, back to the young couple, neither man saying a word, both of them relishing the joy of the long-lost lovers' meeting.

After a few moments, Caleb said, "There is nothing like young love, my Lord."

"No, there is not," Yeshua said, smiling, and he turned to leave.

"Where are you going, my Lord?" Caleb asked.

"I have to get back to Jerusalem. I have a lot to do today."

Caleb reached out and clasped his hands warmly. "Thank you, my Lord."

Yeshua smiled widely, gave a simple nod, and walked away briskly, disappearing into thin air.

Caleb leaned against the fence, watching his beautiful granddaughter. Her bravery and courage had led her here into the light of this new day, and it would be hers to enjoy forever.

The end?

No, it is only the beginning.

Nava is available on Audio at Audible.com
Narrated by Danielle Gensler

Final Things
Could you rate this book with on Amazon?

Review on Amazon
To find me on amazon, search DP Conway books.

Sign Up for my Monthly Newsletter at
dpconway.com
I promise not to annoy you.

Drawing from his Irish American heritage, D.P. Conway weaves faith and hope into his storytelling, exploring the profound mysteries of life and its connection to the Angels and the rest of the unseen Eternal World. His works consistently convey the triumph of light over darkness, inspiring readers to find strength and solace amidst life's trials.

Also by D. P. Conway

Stand Alone Novels
Las Vegas Down
Parkland
The Wancheen
Marisella

The Christmas Collection
Starry Night
The Ghost of Christmas to Come
Nava
Twelve Days
Home for Christmas

Coming Soon
Mary Queen of Hearts
And hopefully many, many, more….

Afterlife Chronicles: Angel Sagas Series
The Epic Series based on Genesis and Revelation
Dawn of Days
Rebellion
Judgment
Empire
The Innocents
And 7 more titles in this epic series.

See many more of D.P. Conway's books on Amazon or visit
www.dpconway.com

Copyright & Publication

Daylights Publishing
5498 Dorothy Drive Suite 3:16
Cleveland, OH 44070

www.dpconway.com
www.daylightspublishing.com

"Nava" is a work of fiction. All incidents, images, dialogue, and all characters, except for some well-known public figures, are products of the author's imagination and are not to be construed as real. Where real-life historical persons, images, or places appear, the situations, incidents, and dialogues concerning those persons are entirely fictional. They are not intended to depict actual events or to change the altogether fictional nature of the work. In all other respects, any resemblance to actual persons, living or deceased, events, institutions, or locales is entirely coincidental.

Cover: Nate Myers
Contributing Story Editor: Colleen Conway Cooper
Copy Editor: Connie Swenson
Proof Reader: Marisa DiRuggiero Conway
Developmental Editor: Caroline Knecht
Audio Narrator: Danielle Gensler

Made in the USA
Middletown, DE
27 October 2023

41468926R00059